THE SPACE SHIP RETURNS
To the Apple Tree

THE SPACE SHIP
RETURNS
TO THE APPLE TREE

LOUIS SLOBODKIN

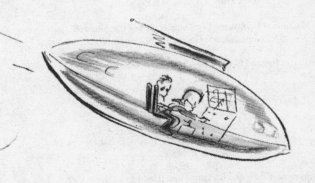

Aladdin Books

Macmillan Publishing Company   *New York*

Maxwell Macmillan Canada   *Toronto*

Maxwell Macmillan International

New York Oxford Singapore Sydney

First Aladdin Books edition 1994
First Collier Books edition 1972
Copyright © 1958 by Louis Slobodkin

Aladdin Books
Macmillan Publishing Company
866 Third Avenue
New York, NY 10022

Maxwell Macmillan Canada, Inc.
1200 Eglinton Avenue East
Suite 200
Don Mills, Ontario M3C 3N1

Macmillan Publishing Company is part of the Maxwell
Communication Group of Companies.

Printed in the United States of America
10 9 8 7 6 5 4 3 2 1

Library of Congress Cataloging-in-Publication Data

Slobodkin, Louis, date.
The space ship returns to the apple tree / Louis Slobodkin. — 1st
Aladdin Books ed.
p.   cm.
Summary: Eddie and his three-foot friend from the planet
Martinea are back together for another summer of adventure.
ISBN 0-689-71768-7
[1. Extraterrestrial beings—Fiction.   2. Science Fiction.]
I. Title.
PZ7.S6333Sn   1994
[Fic]—dc20   93-10747

Contents

CHAPTER ONE

Mysterious Messages

THIS summer when Eddie Blow came up from New York to spend his vacation at his grandmother's apple farm, she was especially glad to see him.

Eddie was now twelve and a half and going to Junior High. He was a Boy Scout, good in Arithmetic, interested in Natural History, very good with electricity, and he wore glasses.

He could rewire and fix almost any electrical appliance that needed fixing. His grandmother always put away a few things during the winter for Eddie to fix during his summer vacation.

This time when Eddie got off the bus from the railroad station, his grandmother was waiting for him on the porch.

And there beside her was a mountain of lamps, radios, electric clocks, kitchen utensils, vacuum cleaners, and so on.

"Hello, Grandma," shouted Eddie, as he ran up the path. "What's the matter? You moving?"

"Hello, Eddie dear," said his grandmother. "My, how you have grown."

"Where you moving, Grandma?" asked Eddie, as he looked around at the pile of things on the porch.

"Moving, Eddie?" said his grandmother. "I'm not moving. You mean about these things here on the porch? Well, come along and wash up. I'll tell you about these things right after you've had your lunch."

After Eddie ate a cold meat sandwich, a banana, and big piece of store cake, his grandmother told him why there were so many things out on the porch.

"It seems," she said, "just about everything that runs by electricity in this house either burnt out, blew up, or ran down. And it's all happened in the past two weeks. A lamp would be working fine then I'd turn it on or off and ph-ph-ph . . . just like that the lamp would blow out or crack or something."

"What happened?" asked Eddie.

"I don't know," said his grandmother. "The same thing happened when I used my toaster or my electric mixer,

8

and even the new electric stove. I was thinking of calling Mr. Marvel, the electrician down in the village, then I figured you'd be coming up here soon and I knew you'd enjoy fixing everything yourself, Eddie. You're always so smart about fixing things."

While she talked, she and Eddie walked out to the porch and looked at the pile of useless electrical appliances. Eddie picked up one of the table lamps, looked at it, turned it upside down, and felt and tugged at the wire. Then he peeked into the electric toaster and tapped it.

"These things look all right, Grandma," he said. "Maybe you just got a short somewhere. Maybe you overloaded your fuses . . ."

"Goodness me, Eddie," said his grandmother, "I'm sure I haven't done anything bad with my fuses. I wouldn't touch the things."

"Tell you what, Grandma," said Eddie, "I'll take these things over to the barn. They won't be hard to fix, I guess."

And Eddie made a few trips to the barn with a wheelbarrow piled up with the things from the porch.

Over in the barn Eddie had a workbench with tools for fixing almost anything. During his summer vacations Eddie spent more time in the barn than he did in the house. Because here in the barn he kept his workbench, tools, and his many collections of stones, arrowheads, and insects. There were not many animals on Eddie's grandmother's farm—just Bessie the cow and her newest calf, the goat, a few geese, chickens and ducks. It was a big barn and there was plenty of room for the animals, the birds, and Eddie with all his collections.

Eddie's grandmother's farm was a large farm on the side of a hill in the upper Hudson River Valley a few miles above Albany. The only things raised on the farm were apples. The soil was too stony for anything else.

The apple trees were sprayed by hired men in the early spring, and when the apples ripened in the fall they were picked, packed and carted away by hired men again. There wasn't much work to do on the farm during the two months Eddie was there. And usually nothing really exciting happened during the long, lazy summer days.

But last summer while Eddie was at the farm one of the most exciting and most unbelievable things happened to him!

10

Last summer Eddie met a little man from OUTER SPACE! He was a Junior Scientist Explorer from the planet Martinea! And he landed his space ship right in Eddie's grandmother's apple orchard!

Of course that is a hard thing to believe and Eddie never told anybody about it because he was sure nobody would believe him.

But it *did* happen!

Eddie got to know the little space man pretty well. And he introduced him to his grandmother. She called the little space man Marty. That was because Eddie's grandmother did not hear too well when Eddie said the little man was a "Mar-tin-ean."

She thought Eddie had said, "Martin E. Ann." That's why she called him Marty which is short for Martin. Eddie never told his grandmother Marty was a space man; it would be too hard to believe.

And when the little space man became earthbound because he lost or mislaid the power which made his space ship fly (he called it Secret Power Z, which is short for Zurianomatichrome), Eddie took him fishing and to a Boy Scout Jamboree and . . .

(But that's another story. There's a book around somewhere called, *The Space Ship under the Apple Tree*, which tells that story.)

And as Eddie pushed the wheelbarrow full of electric toasters, lamps, radios, electric clocks, curling irons, etc., he thought about his friend Marty the space man. He sort of wished something as exciting as Marty's visit would happen again this summer, or that Marty himself might come again.

But of course that was impossible. There was no use wishing for things like that. After all, Marty had returned to the planet Martinea which was millions of miles away.

So Eddie sighed, shrugged his shoulders and went to work on the tangled pile of electric appliances on the barn floor.

The first thing Eddie did was to look at the fuses. The fuse box for the whole farm was right there in the barn. And after taking proper precautions so he would not get a shock (he put on a pair of rubber gloves which he always kept near the fuse box and stood on an old dry rubber bath mat), Eddie opened the fuse box and carefully pulled out the main switch. Then he unscrewed the fuses. He had guessed right. All the fuses were blown out; they had been overloaded. Eddie plugged in some new fuses.

Then in a very short time he inspected and fixed every piece of electrical equipment in the barn.

Most of the lamps just needed new bulbs. Some needed a

little wiring. The toaster and all the kitchen appliances needed very little work. The radio, radio clocks, electric fans, heaters, vacuum cleaners, curling irons and everything else seemed all right.

After Eddie had inspected everything and fixed and rewired everything that needed fixing or rewiring, he plugged them all in one after another into a long string of sockets attached to an extension wire.

Then he opened the fuse box again and he threw the main switch back in again.

Everything worked!

All the lamps lit, the toaster popped, the mixer mixed, the vacuum cleaner whirred, the radio blared, the heater heated, the fans whirred, and everything did what it was supposed to do!

It was just at that moment in the blaze of the lamps and the whirling and blaring of all the other electrical things that Eddie's grandmother, followed by a number of chickens and ducks, opened the barn door!

She raised her hands in surprise and the chickens and ducks ran for their lives—squawking, quacking and cackling!

"HOW'S THAT, GRANDMA!" shouted Eddie, triumphantly above the noise.

"YOU'RE WONDERFUL, EDDIE," screamed his grandmother.

Then she came into the barn quickly and started to turn things off with both hands. The second thing she touched, a lighted lamp, went ph-ph-ph . . . and it was out.

"Guess that was a weak bulb," shouted Eddie.

"Please turn down that radio, Eddie," screamed his grandmother. "I can't hear myself think."

Eddie turned off the radio.

"It was just like I said, Grandma," said Eddie, as he unscrewed the bulb that had gone ph-ph-ph.

"It was the fuses . . . you see, when you use alternating current like you have here on the farm, you gotta watch, I mean, the laws of electrical attraction and repulsion, well, like these fuses, as they . . ."

And while Eddie gave his grandmother a lecture on elec-

14

tricity she went on around the barn pushing buttons and switching things off. Every now and then a lamp would go ph-ph-ph . . . and it was out, or something else would make a strange noise and stop working just as she touched it!

Eddie stopped talking; his mouth hung open as he watched the strange effect his grandmother had on the electric appliances. Some things went right on working after she touched them. Others stopped!

Then he suddenly realized that when she touched something with her *right* hand nothing happened. But when she touched it with her *left* hand it sputtered, ph-ph-ph'd or made some other noise and stopped!

And on her *left* hand she wore a shiny little ring made of a twist of glittering white metal!

Just when she turned around and said, "It will be so nice to have some music coming over my radio again," as she reached out her *left* hand to turn on the radio switch, Eddie shouted:

"DON'T TOUCH THAT RADIO, GRANDMA!"

Eddie's grandmother was startled.

"Eddie," she said, sharply, "whatever is the matter?"

"Grandma," said Eddie, "that ring you're wearing . . . how long have you been wearing that ring?"

"Oh, this ring," said his grandmother with a smile, "you must remember this ring. It's the ring Marty made for me last summer. I found it just a few weeks ago in my button box when I went looking for some buttons to sew on a blouse. It reminded me of Marty and I just slipped it on my finger. You remember, Eddie, when he made this ring for me."

Of course Eddie remembered that ring. He had given Marty, the little space man, a *Boy Scout Manual* and an old American history book and a geography book as a going-

16

away present just before he flew back to his home in Martinea. Marty had given him two presents. One was for Eddie, a Boy Scout pin, and this ring for his grandmother. Marty had made the Scout pin and the ring out of his precious Zurianomatichrome wire, his Secret Power Z. This wire was the secret power that made his space ship fly. And he had told Eddie that Secret Power Z was much more powerful than atomic energy.

Now that's what must have been troubling the electrical appliances, Eddie said to himself. Of course, when Grandma touched anything with her *right* hand nothing happened. But when she touched something with her *left* hand wearing that ring, I bet that Secret Power Z acts as a conductor and overloads the electricity and . . .

"Eddie! Eddie!" said his grandmother, "what are you mumbling? And you're looking so strange!"

"Oh . . . ah . . . I'm sorry, Grandma," said Eddie, "I was just thinking scientifically. Look, I think that ring you're wearing might have something to do with . . . What I mean, it might be the reason the lamps blow out."

"Oh, Eddie," said his grandmother, "how silly. A pretty little ring like this can't hurt anything."

"But Grandma, look, you know, you can make a short and blow out fuses with just a copper penny. Now honestly, I think if you stop wearing that ring . . ."

"Oh, very well, if it will make you any happier, I'll take off Marty's pretty little ring," and she slipped the ring off her finger and dropped it into the pocket of her apron. "Oh, Eddie, what about your little friend Marty? Have you heard from him? Did he write you any letters or did you write him?"

"No, ma'am," said Eddie, "I haven't written any letters to him. I've been sort of busy in school and he hasn't written me either."

"I suppose you both were so busy with school work." Then Eddie's grandmother suddenly interrupted herself. "My pies! Goodness me, my pies are in the oven!" and she ran back to the house as fast as she could go. Just as she turned to run, the little ring made of Zurianomatichrome wire popped out of her pocket and landed on the floor.

Eddie picked up the ring and put it on his workbench.

He went back to work again repairing the lamps and the other things that were damaged by the ring.

Some curious chickens, ducks, and the goat came back and stood in the barn door and watched him work. Most of his wire had been used up and he hunted around in the boxes up on the shelves over his workbench for some more odds and ends of wire. He had some difficulty getting one tight metal box open. And when he finally pried the lid of the box up he gasped!

A strange, bright, bluish light came from the open box!

It was in this box that Eddie kept his most precious and private possessions. In it he kept the telegraph set he had made. Here too were his finest Indian arrowheads. And here was where he had put the *Boy Scout pin made of Zurianomatichrome wire* Marty gave him last summer! Of course, he couldn't wear that pin in New York with his regular Boy Scout uniform. After all, it was not an official Boy Scout pin. And then too it might take an awful lot of explaining.

After the first shock of seeing that strange blue light Eddie understood what had happened. The box and everything in it was charged with Secret Power Z!

He remembered that when Marty had used Secret Power Z to charge all the instruments on his space ship he had inserted the tip of the wire in the little black boxes attached to each instrument. And he remembered too that the inside walls of the space ship itself gave off this same strange blue light because they were also charged with Secret Power Z.

But Eddie knew (because Marty had told him) Secret Power Z was not dangerous or radioactive like atomic energy or anything like that so he was not at all frightened to take the things out of the box.

Everything that was in the box had the blue light—the pin, the arrowheads, and his telegraph set with all its attached wires. He took them out of the box and lay them all very carefully on the workbench.

Eddie tapped the key of his telegraph set a few times. It worked well. Then he switched the little jigger on the set over to receive. The receiving key worked, in fact, it went on working by itself!

That receiving key clicked away just as if he had attached his set to electric wires. And Eddie recognized right away that the telegraph set was charged with Secret Power Z. It was just as if it had its own battery.

He happily went back to work fixing the electric appliances after he found some pretty good wire in another box. The telegraph receiver key went right on cheerfully clicking away. Eddie figured it was just some sort of static and he did not pay much attention to it.

But suddenly he stopped working and listened intently to the clicking telegraph key! It seemed ‾ . . . yes, it did seem . . . that some sort of message was coming through!

There was a regular repeated signal!

Dit . . . dah-di-it . . . dah-di-it . . . di-dit . . . dit!

That was Morse Code!

Eddie dropped what he was doing and rushed over to the workbench to crouch over the busy telegraph key. There it was again, the same signal!

Eddie grabbed a pencil and a piece of paper and waited for the signal to start again. It started and he wrote.

Dit . . . dah-di-it . . . dah-di-it . . . di-dit . . . dit!
  E   D   D   I   E!

That's what the telegraph key was spelling out, his own name, "Eddie!"

"OH! . . . BOY!" shouted Eddie and frightened all the chickens and ducks right out of the barn again but the goat remained.

Eddie waited eagerly now! There it came again over the telegraph receiving key!

Eddie . . . Eddie . . . U.S.A.

Then the rest of the message was lost in a jumble of static. After another long moment the message came again, and this time it was a complete message!

Eddie . . . Eddie . . . U.S.A.
Marty . . . calling . . . Marty . . . calling . . .
Over. . . .

Eddie stared at the message he had written down. His eyes almost popped. Then suddenly he shouted:

"YIPPEE . . . YIPPEE!"

Eddie quickly switched the telegraph set to sending and he clicked out a reply.

Marty . . . Marty . . . This is Eddie . . .
Over. . . .

He switched back to receiving. And he waited and waited and waited, holding his breath.

Then a second message came!

Eddie . . . Eddie . . . U.S.A. . . Marty coming . . .
1 . . . 7 . . . 9 A.M. . . Marty.

Could this really mean that Marty was flying in again from Martinea? What? When? What did he mean by ". . . 1 . . . 7 . . . 9 A.M. . . ?"

The number 1 could be the day and that 7 . . . why that could be the month! The 7th month . . . July! . . . And 9 A.M. . . Why that was perfectly clear!

The 1st of July at 9 A.M. Why, that was tomorrow!

Eddie was so excited he did not know what to do. He switched to sending again and clicked out, "*Marty . . . Marty*" over and over again. But when he switched to receiving there was no response.

He kept the receiving key open waiting for further messages all that afternoon. But nothing happened. The receiving key just clicked and rambled on saying nothing until Eddie's grandmother called him up to the house for supper.

CHAPTER TWO

The Invisible Space Ship

EDDIE slept late the next morning and his grandmother let him sleep.

After all, it was just the second day of his vacation and he had worked so hard fixing the electrical appliances the day before.

But when she finally called up the stairs, "Eddie boy, it's almost nine o'clock . . . Are you going to sleep away this nice, sunny . . . ?" he came rushing down the stairs before she had finished her sentence and raced past her out the front door.

"Eddie! Eddie! What about your breakfast?" she called after him.

He turned just long enough to shout:

"Gotta do something important, Grandma, I'll be back in a few minutes," and he was gone.

Eddie galloped up the road to the apple orchard as fast as he could go. His wrist watch (with a compass on the back of it) which had been given to him on his twelfth birthday said 9:01. If he had understood that message from Marty properly, that meant Marty and his space ship were already here. Where? Up in the apple orchard, of course. That is where Marty had landed in the space ship last summer.

And if he did come again (as Eddie wished terribly hard that he would) he should be up there right now with his space ship hidden near Grandfather's apple tree.

Grandfather's apple tree was the oldest and biggest apple tree in the orchard. It was said that this tree had been planted by Eddie's grandmother's grandfather. The old tree stood high on a ridge overlooking the whole orchard and all the apple trees around were said to be the children, grandchildren and great-grandchildren of Grandfather's apple tree.

Eddie hurried along so fast that he began to pant before he was halfway up the dirt road leading to the tree. This dirt road was a private road that ran through the orchard to the main highway. It was only used by the trucks that carted away the ripe apples in the fall. So Eddie was a little surprised to see a rather small green automobile parked on that section of the road that went alongside the ridge where Grandfather's apple tree grew.

It appeared to be one of those little foreign cars Eddie had often seen on the streets of New York that looked like (so Eddie thought) a slightly overgrown peanut roaster. There was no one in the car or near it. But had there been, Eddie would have said, politely, "Hey you, you know this is a private road. It belongs to my grandmother and no one is allowed to park on it," or something like that.

Eddie told himself that's what he would do later even if Marty came, or if he didn't. He would go looking for the owner of that green peanut roaster and he would say . . . Eddie stopped thinking about that little automobile because he had climbed up to the ridge where Grandfather's apple tree stood.

There was no one there!

Eddie ran around the tree once, then twice more. He looked for the gulley where Marty had hidden his space ship last summer. There was no sign of it and no sign of the space ship or of his friend Marty, the space man!

Sadly, slowly, and quietly, Eddie sat down and leaned back against the trunk of the old tree.

Could he have read that message wrong? He pulled the paper on which he'd scribbled the message out of his pocket. It still said, "Eddie, . . . Eddie . . . U.S.A. Marty coming 1 . . . 7 . . . 9 . . . A.M. . . Marty."

Maybe he had not heard it right! Maybe he had not heard it at all! Since he wanted Marty to come visiting so much, maybe he just imagined that his Secret Power Z charged telegraph set had clicked out the message.

"YOU LATE!" said a stern voice.

Eddie whipped his head around quickly. That voice! Where did it come from? It seemed to come from above! He looked up in the tree.

And there standing on the same branch of the old tree where Eddie first saw him last summer was Marty!

But this time he stood on the top side of the branch. Last summer he had been standing on the bottom side of that branch (held on by his non-gravity shoes) with his head down.

"MARTY!" shouted Eddie.

Marty raised one finger and said, "You late! Now 9:04!"

Marty was not wearing the bright green suit he had worn last summer. He was now wearing a rather strange Boy Scout uniform with a rash of Merit Badges on both sleeves from the wrist right up to the shoulders. Eddie had never seen so many Merit Badges on one Boy Scout. And he never saw a Boy Scout uniform with so many pockets! Marty also wore around his waist a wide button-studded belt. That too was not regulation Boy Scout.

He pressed one of those buttons over his right hip and quickly floated down to the ground.

"Marty! Marty!" cried Eddie. "My old pal Marty."

Marty smiled.

"Friend Eddie," he said. Then he frowned. "What means pal?"

"Oh Marty," said Eddie, "pal means the same as friend. Marty, am I glad to see you!"

Marty smiled again and thrust out his hand. They shook hands warmly using the Boy Scout grip, of course.

"Marty, I don't know what to say. I don't know what to ask you first . . ."

"Ask first," said Marty, "ask first about new heliocopteral disk diminutive."

Marty stood on one foot and stiffly held up his other foot. The shoes he wore were big with buttons and dials along their heavy soles. They looked very much like his last year's non-gravity shoes, except there were round flat disks attached to the soles of the shoes.

"Very modern Martinean style," he said proudly.

Last summer Marty had a small pocket helicopter about as big as a pinwheel that he used to fly short distances. Now Eddie understood he used these little disks or platforms on the bottoms of his shoes for that purpose. And Eddie remembered seeing in newspapers similar one-man platforms . . . larger, of course, that were used by the United States Army. He really was not too impressed with Marty's small flying platforms but he did not say so.

"Where's your space ship?" asked Eddie. "How long

you staying? What you gonna do? When did you become an Eagle Scout?"

Marty held up his hand.

"One question, one answer," he said. "Come."

And he led Eddie down from the ridge to the dirt road, then he stopped. He had stopped near the little green automobile.

"First question answered," said Marty. "Here space ship!"

"WHAT! WHERE?" exclaimed Eddie, whirling around.

Marty was proudly pointing to the little green automobile!

"OH . . . NO, Marty!" cried Eddie, "that *can't* be your space ship."

Marty grinned and nodded.

"Yes, space ship . . . very modern Martinean Interspacial Superphotic Astral Rocket Disk. This space ship made from special metal for me by Martinean scientist. This metal named Bamboozelergical Metal."

"But Marty, that looks like one of those peanut roasters . . ."

Marty reached into one of his many pockets and took out a little flat box. It was no bigger than a pill box. He held it up in front of his mouth and said, "Peanut roaster." The face of the box lit up and strange little markings whirled across the box. Then the little marks stood still. Marty

knitted his brows as he read:

"Peanuts . . . U.S.A. . . . Vegetable Bean Family . . . Peanut Roaster . . . Roaster to roast peanuts."

He turned the face of the box to Eddie. Eddie saw that the marks were words written with the Martinean alphabet. He had seen Marty scribble something on a blackboard in his space ship last summer. Of course, Eddie could not read Martinean.

"This new Auto-Translation Dictionary say wrong?" asked Marty. "New design maybe no work."

(Last year Marty had used a dictionary box to translate English into Martinean.)

"No, that's right," said Eddie, "that's what a peanut roaster is. Yeh, a peanut roaster is for roasting peanuts. But I really didn't mean that your space ship looks like a peanut roaster . . . it looks like a . . . ."

"This space ship," interrupted Marty with an angry voice,

"is designed for disguise. Must look like automobile . . . not peanut roaster! Martinean scientists make no mistake."

"Oh, Marty . . . I'm sorry . . . sure, that's what I mean," said Eddie, hastily. "It does look like a little automobile. I just meant . . ."

Marty smiled again. He held up one hand to quiet Eddie, then he dipped again into one of his many pockets and brought out two pair of (what looked like) rose-tinted sun glasses. He gave Eddie one pair and told him to put them on while he put on the other pair. After Eddie had put the rose-tinted sun glasses on top of his own glasses, Marty again pointed towards the little green automobile.

The little green automobile had disappeared!

In its place stood the handsomest, sleekest, space ship Eddie had ever seen.

"Oh, boy, Marty. She's a peach! That's the prettiest space ship I ever saw."

Marty was so proud, his chest swelled way out.

"But Marty, how come I didn't see it?"

Marty held up his hand again.

"Understand question," he said.

Then he quickly explained that this space ship, this brand-new Interspacial Superphotic Astral Rocket Disk was designed especially for Marty as a prize because he had given such a good report about his visit to the United States last summer.

The space ship was made of two Bamboozelergical metals. These were very remarkable metals recently discovered in Martinea. One of these metals resisted the visual light rays. It could not be seen except with these special visualizers that Eddie and Marty now wore. This metal became completely transparent in daylight. The other metal did not resist visual light rays. It could be seen by everybody and it was very strong but it could fold up like paper.

The outer walls and all the instruments of the space ship were made of this transparent visual ray resisting metal. The little green automobile which was really in the center of the space ship was made of the strong folding metal that everybody could see.

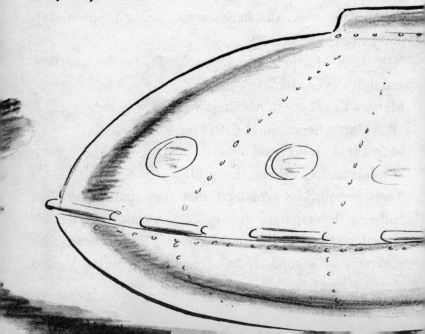

That's why Eddie saw only the little green automobile until he put on the visualizers, the rose-tinted sun glasses.

"Good disguise for space ship . . . No?" asked Marty.

Eddie was speechless!

Then Marty answered the second question Eddie had asked. What was Marty doing on this second visit to Earth? He told Eddie this time he was really going to explore the United States of America. On his last visit because he had lost the Secret Power Z, he had spent his whole time on the planet Earth on Eddie's grandmother's farm or near it. He had been able to give his prize-winning report on his visit

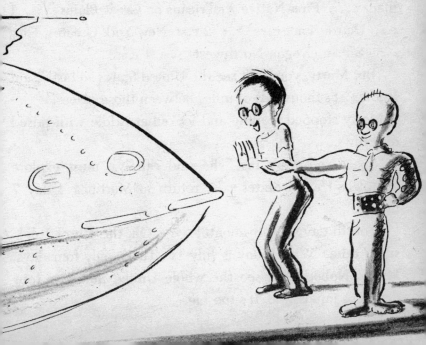

only because his friend Eddie had told him so much about the United States and because he had read the books . . . the *Boy Scout Manual* and the old school books Eddie had given him as a going-away present.

Now with this new well-disguised modern space ship he could travel any place he wanted to go in the United States. Then Marty asked Eddie if he wanted to go exploring with him.

"Exploring!" exclaimed Eddie. "Exploring where?"

"All United States," said Marty. He pulled a little card out of one of his pockets and he read off "1 day 7 month 11 A.M. . . Go to Washington, D.C. . . 12 P.M. Go see Indians . . . First Native Americans on Great Plains . . . 1 P.M. Detroit Factories . . . 2 P.M. New York Greatest City . . . 3 P.M. Oregon Northwest . . . 4 P.M. . ."

"But Marty, you can't see the United States so fast!" said Eddie. "It's thousands of miles between those places."

Marty stopped reading and looked at Eddie with raised eyebrows.

"Space ship very fast," he said calmly, "must explore complete United States . . . return to Martinea 4 day 7 month."

"Fourth day seventh month? . . . Oh, the 4th of July!" said Eddie. "Why, today is July 1st. That's only four days, Marty. Nobody can see the whole United States in four days. It's impossible. It's too big."

"Saw whole United States in four seconds," said Marty.

"Now how did you see the whole United States in four seconds?" asked Eddie, impatiently.

Marty pointed one finger straight up.

"From space ship," he said, "coming to Earth."

"Oh," said Eddie, "what I mean you can't cover all that ground in just a few days."

"Can do," said Marty. "Will come explore?"

"We-e-l-l . . . I don't know," said Eddie, "I'll have to ask my grandmother . . ." Then Eddie interrupted himself, "O-o-h . . . My grandmother! I forgot I gotta go, Marty. I promised my grandmother I'd be back for breakfast in a few minutes."

Eddie looked at his wrist watch.

"Say . . . It's only 9:30. Look, Marty, why don't you come down and have breakfast too. My grandmother likes you. She asked about you just yesterday. We'll eat quick."

Marty took a little shiny spiky metal instrument out of one of his pockets. He held it up towards the sun, then he said: "Time now . . . 1 . . . 7 . . . 9:29 . . . your time wrong . . . yes, can eat breakfast."

And while Eddie turned his wrist watch back one minute, Marty took hold of Eddie's elbow with one hand and with his other he pressed one of the buttons on his belt and Z-i-p . . . they were standing on Eddie's grandmother's front porch!

CHAPTER THREE

The Explorers

"MARTY, I do declare!" Eddie's grandmother threw her hands up high with delight when Marty and Eddie walked in the door, "my cup runneth over. Here Eddie just came yesterday and here you are too. I'm very happy to see you."

Marty smiled and thrust out his hand. He really liked Eddie's grandmother. After shaking his hand with both of her hands, Eddie's grandmother said:

"Sit down and have breakfast with us. We're having apple pancakes with cherry jam. They're ready to eat now."

Eddie's grandmother did all the talking as he and Marty ate their breakfast. They just nodded or shook their heads when she asked a question. Eddie could not tell whether Marty nodded or shook his head when Eddie's grandmother asked Marty what did he do to get so many decorations on his Boy Scout uniform (she meant Merit Badges, of course).

Eddie wondered about that too. How *did* Marty get some of those Merit Badges? Marty wore more Merit Badges on his uniform than any Scout Eddie ever knew. The ones he had for "Astronomy," "Aeronautics," "Airplane Design," "Aerodynamics," and things like that were completely understandable. But how did Marty get the ones for "Hog and Pork Production," "Leather Work," "Taxidermy," "Sheep Farming," and "Nut Culture?"

Marty never spoke of Martinean animals. Did they have pigs up in Martinea? And did they have nuts?

Somehow Eddie managed to slide in a question while his grandmother stopped talking to take a breath.

"Grandma, do you mind if I go exploring?" he asked. "Marty asked me to go exploring with him. He isn't gonna be here long . . ."

"Of course, you can go exploring, Eddie," said his grandmother. "I tell you what. I'll put up some sandwiches for both of you, so you can have your lunch out. Now it'll take just a minute . . . then you can have a nice, long day exploring . . . Marty, you come back with Eddie for supper. We're having fried chicken."

Marty nodded. Eddie raced up the stairs and got into his Boy Scout uniform while his grandmother made the sandwiches. He felt more like an explorer dressed as a Boy

Scout. And in a few minutes he and Marty were hurrying up the road again towards the orchard. Eddie carried the sandwiches in his knapsack. Marty did not put on too much speed as they left the house. He held on to Eddie's elbow, pressed a button on his belt and Eddie found himself taking long steps. His feet hardly touched the ground.

When they reached the turn in the road where Eddie's grandmother, who had been waving good-bye could no longer see them, Marty pressed another button and Z-i-p . . . they were standing alongside the little green automobile again.

"Marty," said Eddie, "you're not really going to try to go to Washington and Oregon and places like that all in one day, are you?"

"Yes, very easy to do," said Marty. "Put on visualizers."

And as Marty spoke he put on the rose-tinted sun glasses and Eddie put the pair he had on top of his own glasses again.

Once more the little green automobile disappeared and in its place stood the beautiful space ship.

It was not taller than the little green automobile. And it was about ten feet in diameter. There was a line of porthole windows around the ship and on the outer brim a chain of small tubes. They were similar to the tubes that were on Marty's last space ship. Eddie knew they were rocket tubes.

Marty stood very close to the space ship and faced it. Then he said a Martinean word. It sounded like "Punepo!" A narrow door appeared in the wall of the space ship. Marty turned to Eddie and with a proud smile said, "Follow."

They had to crouch down as they went into the space ship. This one was a lot smaller than the ship Marty had used last summer.

As soon as he entered the space ship, Marty pushed a button near the door and the little green automobile folded up and slid down into the floor of the space ship. And the steering wheel collapsed and folded into the wall of the space ship. All that was left of the little green automobile were the two seats.

In front of the seats there was an instrument panel with all sorts of gadgets on it. And on the wall of the space ship there were a lot of levers, buttons, and knobs. Right over the seats there was some sort of map or geographical chart. It looked something like the United States but not exactly.

Marty climbed into one seat, then motioned for Eddie to sit in the other. After they were seated Marty turned towards the open door and said, "Esolc!"

The little door slid into place and it fit so tightly into place Eddie could not see where the doorway had been. The space ship wall looked completely solid.

Of course Eddie had never flown in a space ship before.

He had never even been up in any kind of an airplane except the little tin ones that were attached to merry-go-rounds. Once he did have a ride hanging from a parachute . . . one of those ten-cent-a-ride parachutes that slide down a long wire out in Coney Island. He found he was getting just a little nervous at the thought of going up in a space ship.

Maybe, he said to himself, he ought to tell Marty that he would like a ride in his space ship on some other day. Out of the corner of his eye he looked at Marty.

Marty was frowning as he studied the instrument board in front of him. He reached forward one finger and after a little hesitation he poked one of the buttons on the board. He seemed quite surprised when some little jigger on the right side wall of the space ship began to buzz and whirl.

He hastily pushed that same button again and the jigger stopped whirling and buzzing. Then after another moment's thought he pushed another button. And on the left side of the space ship a number of little lights began to flash on and off. Quickly Marty pushed that button again and the lights stopped.

Marty took a small luminous book out of one of his pockets. He opened it and studied the markings in it for a while. Then he turned a small knob on the instrument board. This time he seemed pleased with the result. The chart overhead lit up.

He turned to Eddie and pointed to the dial and the chart, "This Automatic Synchronized Pilot . . . Set flight to destination . . . Space ship fly direct . . . This very new space ship. Must study operation more."

"Aren't you sure how it works yet, Marty?" asked Eddie nervously.

Marty did not answer him. He had found something else in the little book that he wanted to know.

That must be a book of instructions on How to Fly a Space Ship, Eddie said to himself, and out loud he said,

"Look, Marty, maybe I ought not go with you today. Maybe you should go exploring yourself. There are some things I ought to do here on the farm."

Marty wasn't listening to him. He reached forward again and turned a small lever. And while Eddie was still talking, a padded metal band swung around from the back of the seat and before Eddie knew it he found himself clamped tight in his seat. A metal band had surrounded Marty too.

Then Marty looked up at the chart overhead, turned a dial that made a long thin needle on the chart vibrate and at last he turned his head and spoke to Eddie.

"What you said?" he asked.

"I was thinking . . . Is this the first time you ever flew this space ship, Marty?"

"No," said Marty, "second time . . . First time from Martinea."

Eddie gulped.

"Maybe . . . I don't think I ought to fly today, Marty. I'll be glad to fly with you tomorrow. There are some things . . . You know what, I think I'll get out . . ."

"Too late," said Marty, "flying now."

Eddie's heart jumped up into his throat!

The take-off had been so smooth he had not even felt it. He looked out the portholes of the space ship and all he could see was clear, dark blue sky.

"Flying above iconosphere. One thousand miles above earth surface," said Marty, in a matter-of-fact voice. "This fine space ship, fly by instruments alone. Next stop Washington, D.C."

"Oh, Marty," said Eddie, "you should have told me."

"HOLD BREATH!" shouted Marty, "we dive to landing in Washington, D.C.!"

Eddie had just about enough time to take a deep breath and shut his mouth when he felt a gentle bump. He turned his head to look out the porthole over the rims of his rose-tinted glasses. And he saw green trees.

"Here . . . Washington, D.C.!" said Marty.

CHAPTER FOUR

The Thousand Mile Mistake

THE moment the space ship landed, the little green automobile unfolded and automatically came up around Marty and Eddie from the floor of the space ship. The padded metal bands that had clamped them to their seats snapped back into place.

Anyone who now looked at the space ship through its transparent visual resisting outer walls saw what appeared to be just two boys sitting in a little green automobile.

Marty took off his visualizers and so did Eddie. They looked through the windows of the little automobile and through the transparent outer walls of the space ship. They had landed on a wide, very sunny street.

"What you gonna see first here in Washington?" asked Eddie.

"Capitol building of United States of America," said Marty, promptly.

"Well, we'd better get out and ask somebody where it is," said Eddie. "I've never been to Washington before."

Marty was surprised and a little shocked.

"You never saw Capital City of your United States?" he asked.

Eddie shook his head.

"You see now," said Marty, and he climbed out of the disguised space ship followed by Eddie.

It was very hot out on that wide sunny street. There were not many people walking along and there were very few automobiles. They looked up and down the street for a moment.

A big automobile driven by a big policeman pulled up alongside of the little green automobile. The policeman climbed out and looked into the green automobile, then he spoke to Marty and Eddie.

"Did you boys see the driver of this little automobile?"

Eddie pointed to Marty.

"Well, Scout. You have been driving on the wrong side of the street. You'll have to turn your car around. I won't give you a ticket this time but don't let it happen again."

Marty half-covered his mouth with his hand and whispered to Eddie, "Who this man?"

"He's a policeman, Marty. The Law!" Eddie whispered back. "You'd better turn the space ship around right away, Marty, if you can."

Marty nodded, "You talk with policeman," he whispered.

"Come on now, Scout," said the big policeman, "it's hot standing out in this sun. Get into that little car and turn it around."

Marty nodded and climbed back into the disguised space ship. Eddie walked over and stood between the space ship and the policeman.

"It sure is a scorcher today," said the big policeman. He took a handkerchief out of his pocket, then he took his hat off and rubbed the handkerchief over his bald head and down his red face.

In that instant as his handkerchief was passing over his face, Marty whirled the space ship high up into the air and brought it down again!

"Come on now, boy," said the policeman impatiently, "are you gonna turn that car? Oh, you did turn it. You're a good driver, Scout."

Then Eddie asked the policeman where they could find the Capitol. Marty came out of the space ship and stood by his side.

"The old Capitol, eh? Sure, I'll tell you how to get to the Capitol. It's just a short distance. But if you're gonna drive, this is a one-way street so you'll have to go back and turn . . ."

"We're gonna walk," said Eddie firmly, after he took one quick look at Marty.

"Sure, that's the best way. Now you just walk along this street just three blocks. Then turn right, remember that, right, not left, and you'll see the old Capitol right in front of you."

"Thank you," said Eddie.

"Think nothing of it," said the big policeman with a generous wave of his hand.

Marty and Eddie walked along at a regular pace. Marty did not put on any speed.

"You know, Marty," said Eddie, "I didn't think Washington was going to look like this. Somehow from the pictures I saw . . . Where do you want to go after we see the Capitol?"

Marty reached into one of his pockets, brought out a card and read a list of the places he wanted to see as he walked along.

"Mr. Smith Sons' Institute . . . Congress Library . . . The White Painted House . . ."

"Wait a minute, Marty," said Eddie. "Do you mean the Smithsonian Institution?"

Marty nodded.

". . . And the Library of Congress?"

Marty nodded again.

". . . And the White House where the President lives?"

And for the third time Marty nodded his head.

"If we're gonna see all those places here in Washington maybe we ought to hurry up a little," said Eddie.

And as soon as he said that he was sorry. Because Marty took his elbow, pressed a button on his belt, and Z-i-p . . . they flew down the street and swung around the corner— and almost knocked down an elderly man who was coming along that street.

Eddie quickly apologized for both of them (Marty nodded).

"What's all this hurry?" grumbled the elderly man as he straightened out his straw hat. "Rushing around like crazy on a hot day."

"We're in a hurry to see the Capitol," said Eddie.

"The Capitol!" exclaimed the man, "why, that old Capitol has been standing there a long time and it will be waiting for you."

"Standing where?" asked Eddie. He turned and looked every which way. He had seen photographs, drawings, paintings, moving pictures and even embroidered pillow covers that pictured the domed Capitol of the United States but none of those buildings on either side of this street looked like the Capitol.

"Right there, boy, use your eyes," and the elderly man poked his cane at a rather ramshackle building set back from the street.

The building had a broad rickety veranda with a wooden sign suspended from its roof. There once had been some words painted on that sign. But now the paint had peeled and no one could read what it said.

"There she stands, the old Capitol Hotel! Maybe one of the oldest hotels in this part of Florida!"

"The Capitol Hotel? Florida?" gasped Eddie. "What part of Florida?"

"Why, Miami Beach, Florida. What's the matter with you, boy? Gotta touch of sun?"

Eddie turned to Marty and hoarsely whispered, "Did you hear that, Marty? We're in Florida! We by-passed Washington by almost a thousand miles!"

50

"What's that?" asked the old man cupping one hand around his ear. "Washington? Are you Washington people? We get a lot of Washington people down here. Thousands."

But Eddie was not listening. He looked at Marty. And Marty with his mouth open was stiff and staring as if he'd been turned to stone.

Suddenly he snapped out of it and mumbled, "Small mistake."

Then with one hand he grabbed Eddie's elbow and with the other he pushed a button on his belt and Z-i-p . . . they were back at the space ship, in it, and they blasted off into space again before the elderly man had picked up his straw hat! His hat had been blown off by the breeze they stirred up when they left him.

CHAPTER FIVE

Sticko to the Rescue

MARTY was very flustered because he had missed Washington by almost a thousand miles. And he fussed and twiddled with the buttons, dials and gadgets in the space ship without saying a word after they took off. At last he twisted the dial of the Automatic Synchronized Pilot and set the needle on the overhead chart and again said, "Next stop Washington, D.C."

He sounded sad. So Eddie tried to think of something to cheer him up.

"Everybody can make a small mistake, Marty, maybe you ought to study that instruction book on how to fly this new space ship a little more."

Marty frowned and did not say anything. After about a minute he reached into one of his pockets and brought

52

out the little luminous book and opened it up. Suddenly he looked up from the book to the chart overhead. Then he looked back into his book again. Then back to the chart! Then he quickly reached up and twisted the dial that made the long needle on the chart spin. He turned the dial back and forth a few times but the needle on the chart did not move!

"Stuck," he said angrily. He kept working at the dial and nothing happened. That long needle did not budge a speck!

Eddie stole a look at the little compass on the back of the wrist watch he had received on his twelfth birthday. He did not want Marty to know that he was using such an old-fashioned instrument in his brand new Interspacial Superphotic Astral Rocket Disk. The tiny needle in the little compass said that they were flying due north.

Marty kept on working on the Automatic Synchronized Pilot. He twisted and retwisted the dial and then in a fit of impatience, he gave it a yank! The thing came off in his hand!

He tried desperately to push the dial back onto its socket but it would not stay. It kept falling off again and again. He turned and looked at Eddie helplessly.

"You want me to help, Marty?" asked Eddie. "I gotta tube of Sticko. It sticks anything together, paper, glue, glass, . . ."

Marty frowned and shook his head. He pushed the dial onto its socket and tried to hammer it back with the palm of his hand.

Eddie took another quick look at his little compass. It still said due north and it was getting cooler in that space ship!

The space ship had felt cool after the hot Miami sun but now it was definitely cooler. In fact, it was getting cold and getting colder with each passing second. Marty had not yet got that dial back where it belonged and the space ship still flew with tremendous speed . . . due north!

Eddie hunted around in his pocket for the tube of Sticko. He unscrewed the cap of the tube and held it ready in case Marty changed his mind and decided to use it.

And just as the temperature in the space ship sank from very, very, very cold to freezing to sub-zero, Marty grabbed the tube of Sticko from Eddie's hand, squirted some Sticko on the socket of the dial and slapped the dial back into place!

THE STICKO WORKED! THE DIAL STUCK!

At last Marty regained control of the Automatic Synchronized Pilot and not a moment too soon!

The long needle on the overhead chart trembled! It twitched! It moved! The space ship tilted sharply and changed course!

It seemed they were flying rather low. For just a split second through the porthole windows Eddie saw something that might have been jagged peaks of ice!

On one ice peak rounder and taller than the others, there was a ragged American flag!

The tiny magnetic needle on Eddie's little compass acted sort of crazy. It whirled round and round and then back and forth.

Now Marty leaned back in his seat again and was cheerful.

"Next stop Washington, D.C.," he said, confidently.

Eddie looked quickly at his compass. The little needle acted normal again. They *were* heading south once more.

"Marty," said Eddie, his voice trembling, "was that the North Pole?"

Marty did not answer him. He found things to do on the instrument board. He kept himself very busy until he shouted, "Hold breath for landing!"

But Eddie did not hold his breath. Instead he shouted: "DON'T!"

Marty quickly leaned forward, pushed a button and the space ship swooped up into the air again. He turned to Eddie.

"Now look here, Marty," said Eddie, "you can't just go and land any place. You gotta pick a spot. What if you come down on the White House lawn? The F.B.I. or the soldiers will shoot you or something."

Marty nodded.

"You right," he said, and he touched another gadget on the instrument board and the space ship whirled around in a wide circle.

"Take off visualizers," said Marty, as he took off his rose-tinted glasses.

They were able to look down through the floor of the now transparent space ship. Eddie felt a little squeamish whirling around in space like that with nothing between him and the earth but thousands of feet of thin air and the folded up little automobile under their feet. He had taken off his visualizers and he could see through the transparent floor and walls of the space ship.

Marty took a tiny but powerful telescope from one of his pockets and looked down through the floor of the space ship.

"Where good place for landing?" he asked Eddie, passing the telescope to him.

Eddie looked through the telescope. How large everything looked! Everything was so close that he felt he could just reach out his hand and pick up crumpled chewing gum wrappers right off the streets. He saw a number of cars lined up in a fenced in lot. It was a parking lot!

"There's a good place," said Eddie. "It's a parking lot. Look, Marty, straight down, see those cars?"

Marty took the telescope, found the parking lot and then he pushed a button and shouted, "Hold breath! Dive for landing."

The space ship dropped like a shot. It landed neatly between two large trucks in the parking lot.

A man sprawling in a chair and reading a newspaper looked up as Eddie and Marty walked towards the gate of the parking lot.

"Hey, you kids," he said, "you can't go running through this place. This is no empty lot to play in. It's a place of business. Moriarty's Parking Lot. And I'm Moriarty."

"We just parked our car," said Eddie.

"How come? I didn't see you come into the lot. Where did you park it? You know you gotta pay for parking here."

Eddie and Marty led Mr. Moriarty over to the little green automobile (the disguised space ship) between the two big trucks.

Mr. Moriarty looked at the little green car a moment.

"Oh, that," he said. "Well, we charge 75¢ an hour for parking real cars here. Tell you what, I'll charge you ten cents for that."

Eddie started to dig around in his pockets. He had two nickels mixed up with some string and a few other things he usually carried in his pockets.

"You don't pay me now," said Mr. Moriarty, "pay when you get your car out. Here's your ticket. And would you want your car washed while it's here?"

Marty who had been silent until then shouted: "NO!"

"All right. Keep calm," said Mr. Moriarty, "don't get

excited. I know it doesn't look as if it needs a washing. But I ask everybody. Just force of habit, I guess."

Eddie understood why Marty got excited. It seems that Earth Moisture (water, dew, lemon pop, or any of the Earth's liquids) spoils the machines made in Martinea. Last summer Marty's Secret Power Z (Zurianomatichrome wire) was just about ruined by being dunked in a brook. He edged Marty towards the gate and they left the parking lot.

Marty and Eddie walked briskly along the busy street. There were a lot of people and a lot of automobiles on that street and Marty did not push any buttons in his belt for special speed.

At the first corner they came to, Eddie read the name of the street that they were walking on. It was printed up on a lamppost . . . "Washington Street."

"See that," he said to Marty. "Washington Street."

Marty nodded.

Somehow this city looked more like Washington ought to look, Eddie said to himself. He should have known the moment that they landed in Miami, Florida, that it was not Washington. The pictures he had seen of parades along the Washington streets never showed any dusty green palm trees such as they saw in Miami.

Of course he realized they were now in the business district. But he was sure they would soon find the Capitol,

Library of Congress and everything else Marty wanted to see, or if they did not, they would ask someone.

Yes, these streets were more like the streets he expected to see in Washington . . . big buildings . . . old churches. They had just passed an old church. There was a bronze plaque on it with some words printed: "Old South Church 1730–1782". . . . Old South Church?

That struck a bell in Eddie's mind. The Old South Church? It had something to do with the Revolutionary War. Wasn't that where the lanterns were hung in the tower for Paul Revere? . . . "one if by land, two if by sea". . . No!

That was the Old North Church! Eddie always mixed up the Old South Church and the Old North Church.

The Old South Church was where the Patriots met and dressed up as Indians and dumped the British tea into the Boston Harbor! Sure, the Boston Tea Party!

BOSTON!???

Then Eddie saw a sign that confirmed his suspicion. It was on the window of a store, "Boston Shoe Store . . . The Best Shoes in Boston."

THIS WAS BOSTON!

They were not in Washington at all!

They walked on in silence for a few blocks. Eddie worried how he could tell Marty that he had made another "small

60

mistake" today . . . that his space ship had missed Washington again.

Marty, who had been walking along cheerfully looking up at the buildings, stopped abruptly. He took out the shiny, spiky little instrument he used to tell time and held it up to the sun and said:

"Now 1 day 7 month . . . 12:01 P.M. . . Where is Capitol, Congress Library . . ." and Marty ran down the list of the places he had planned to see in Washington. ". . . Is late now."

"Is it that late?" said Eddie, as he still tried to figure some way he could break the news to Marty that they were not in Washington. "I tell you what, Marty, let's eat our lunch now. There, see that park. Let's go over into that park. And the minute we get done with lunch we'll ask somebody where we can find places . . ."

Marty thought a moment, then he nodded his head.

They found a bench and settled down to their lunch. Eddie's grandmother had packed about a dozen big sandwiches in Eddie's knapsack . . . cold roast beef sandwiches and peanut butter and currant jelly sandwiches.

After Marty had eaten three sandwiches (one roast beef and two peanut butter and currant jelly), and after he had started on his fourth sandwich Eddie gently broke the news to him that another "small mistake" had been made. The space ship had landed about five hundred miles short of Washington.

"Marty," he said, "have you ever heard of Boston?"

Marty chewed his fourth sandwich slowly . . . then he nodded.

"Boston . . . Mass. . . Cradle American History . . ." He seemed to be reciting from memory. He stopped and hunted around with jelly stained fingers in one of his pockets until he found a card.

"Yes . . . Boston Mass. Cradle American History . . .

home of Bean and Cod . . . explore Boston . . . 3 day 7 month . . . 10 A.M. . . See Massachusetts Institute Technology, Harvard University, Boston Public Library, Copley Square, Old South Church, Old North Church, Paul Revere House, . . ."

(It was evident Marty had read very carefully the history and geography books Eddie had given to him last summer.)

"Yeh . . . I know, I know," Eddie interrupted. "I read those books too. Look, Marty, since you were going to explore Boston anyhow . . . Huh? It really doesn't matter too much . . ."

Marty, who had taken another bite of the sandwich, stopped chewing and looked at Eddie.

"What I mean, Marty . . . Maybe you ought to go to Boston and all the other places on your card . . . before you go to Washington."

Marty swallowed his mouthful.

"Why?" he asked.

"Well, Marty, . . . Have you got a passport?"

Marty shook his head. "What is passport?"

"A passport. Huh, well . . . It's like this. If somebody comes from some other place to the United States, that person's gotta have a passport and a visiting permit. Now you haven't got a passport or a visiting permit, have you?"

Marty shook his head.

Eddie had found out about passports when he went to the United Nations building in New York with his Boy Scout troop. He had met Boy Scouts from foreign lands there. They talked about passports, visiting permits, and things like that.

"Well, you see . . . Now since you haven't any of those things, it might be better if you explore other places first before you . . . I mean, it would be better to explore places like Boston for instance. I think they're very strict about passports in Washington. After all, that's the capital of the United States. The President lives there and Congress and the F.B.I. and the U.S. Treasury . . ."

Marty sat there with his mouth open. Suddenly he interrupted.

"But this city *is* Washington!" he insisted.

"H-u-h . . . H-m-m . . . Well, no, Marty," said Eddie, very gently. "This is not Washington . . . this is Boston."

Marty frowned and thought for a long minute. And then to Eddie's complete amazement and great relief he nodded.

"All right . . . explore Boston first."

"O.k.," cried Eddie, "let's go."

CHAPTER SIX

Special Speed

In just about a half hour Marty (with Eddie tagging along) had explored Boston very thoroughly. Marty used his special speed very discreetly. With one hand on Eddie's elbow and the other on the speed-up buttons on his belt, he would move normally while other people were watching. But as soon as the coast was clear he and Eddie whirled through the streets or through buildings with a Z-i-p.

And all the time Marty kept turning his head from side to side. Sometimes he surprised dignified Boston ladies by appearing alongside of them as they peered at some historical relics in a museum and then disappearing again before they could catch their breath.

At a special exhibition of Advanced Automatic Calculating Machines at the Massachusetts Institute of Technology

65

Marty whirled in and out of the place so fast that many of the complicated machines that were there were put out of order for quite a few minutes after he left.

As they left every building or anything else he had wanted to see, Marty would stop for a second and pull out a little silver colored box. It was round and just about an inch long. He pushed a little plunger on one side of the box, then he talked into it very rapidly in Martinean language. And then he'd snap it back into his pocket and they were off again.

When Eddie asked about the box Marty graciously stopped for two seconds. He explained that he was recording his report of what he saw while he explored. And he pushed the little plunger and showed Eddie how it worked.

"Speak," he said, holding the silver box up to Eddie's mouth.

"What'll I say?" asked Eddie.

"Anything," said Marty.

"I can't think of anything."

"Speak!" insisted Marty.

"Oh, all right . . . h-m-m . . . Boston Beans. Boston Beans, Boston Beans," said Eddie into the silver box.

Then Marty pushed a plunger on the other side of the silver box and held it up to Eddie's ear.

The box spoke! It said:

"SpeakWhat'llIsayAnythingIcan'tthinkofanythingSpeak OhallrightHmmmBostonBeansBostonBeansBostonBeans!"

"Was that my voice?" asked Eddie.

Marty nodded and they were off again.

At last, right after they had a ride on one of the Swan Boats in the Public Gardens pond (Marty pushed one of his speed-up buttons and that Swan Boat really ripped through the water), he decided he had enough of Boston.

"Now," he said, "return to space ship."

"Oh, Marty," said Eddie, "I forgot to get the address of that parking lot. We'd better get a telephone book. It was Mr. Moriarty's parking lot. We'll find it in the book. Don't worry."

Marty smiled and shook his head.

"Not necessary," he said. He took hold of Eddie's elbow and pressed a large button in the front of his belt. He had not pressed that button until now. Eddie and Marty moved along the street at a reasonable pace and turned proper

corners until they were back at Mr. Moriarty's parking lot.

Marty explained as they moved along that the large button was an Automatic Returnascope. It was on a direct Superconiatic Beam to the space ship. All he ever had to do when he went exploring away from the space ship was to press this button and automatically he returned to his space ship.

And Marty and Eddie floated happily along (at medium speed) through the Boston streets until they came to the gate of Mr. Moriarty's parking lot.

There was some sort of commotion going on there. Mr. Moriarty and two men (one tall and thin . . . the other short and wide) were having an argument over in the corner where Marty had parked his space ship.

"Listen here, Moriarty," growled the tall, thin man, poking a finger into Mr. Moriarty's chest, "if I don't get my truck out of here in just ten minutes I'll never park my truck here again."

"And that goes for me too," shouted the short wide man.

Mr. Moriarty was angry. He waved his arms in the air.

"But I told you and I told you and I told you," he stormed, "I can't move that green baby carriage of an automobile. It's locked up and I haven't got the keys."

Marty and Eddie stood quietly watching the men argue. It seemed that the little green automobile had been parked between the two trucks so that neither of them could back out and drive away from their place in the parking lot. Eddie wanted to say something but Marty touched his elbow and held him back.

"Now here's my ultimatum," shouted the short, wide man, banging the fist of one hand into the palm of the other. "If that lizard-green tin can is not out of my way before I count three, I'm going to get into my truck and I'll back up and I'll smash the livin' daylights out of it."

"Keep calm now, keep calm," shouted Mr. Moriarty. "Don't go threatening to ruin any of my customers' private property or . . ."

The tall, thin man interrupted.

"What are we wasting time for," he said to the smaller man. "If he can't drive that two by four green tin can out of our way, let's just pick it up and throw it out of the way."

Eddie started again to move forward but Marty still held his arm and shook his head.

The tall thin man and the short wide man rushed at the little automobile.

"Careful now, careful!" shouted Mr. Moriarty.

But he did not have to worry. The truckmen did not touch the little green car. They rushed at it from opposite sides and since they could not see the invisible walls of the space ship, they slapped up against the outside rim

of the space ship and fell flat on its transparent walls. Then they slid off onto the ground.

"I must have stumbled," said the tall, thin man.

"I bumped myself too," grumbled the short, wide man. "Get on your feet and let's try again."

And just as they started to go for the little automobile once more, Marty gave Eddie a little push towards Mr. Moriarty. Eddie stumbled forward.

"Hello. We're back," said Eddie. He could not think of anything else to say.

Mr. Moriarty swung around.

"So you're back," he said, "and with the trouble you and your green tin kettle of a car has given me I wish . . ."

"What do we owe you for parking?" interrupted Eddie.

"You owe me nothing," cried Mr. Moriarty, and he pointed to the gate. "Just get your little green four-wheeled monster out of this parking lot. You're ruining my business."

The tall, thin man and the short wide man climbed up into the cabs of their trucks.

"Get moving," shouted the tall, thin man.

"Pull out," shouted the short, wide man.

Marty and Eddie quickly climbed into the little green automobile. And Mr. Moriarty backed away to direct the movement of all three automobiles.

The moment Marty and Eddie were back in the space ship, Marty pushed the Maximum Speed Ascending button and before the truckmen had even turned the keys to start their motors the space ship was over 50,000 feet in the air.

Marty kept the space ship hovering over the parking lot for just a moment while he looked down through his powerful telescope. He smiled and passed the telescope to Eddie so that he too could see Mr. Moriarty and the truckmen down there in the parking lot still angrily waiting for Marty to drive the little green automobile out the gate.

CHAPTER SEVEN

Secret Power ZZZ

THE space ship cruised around in wide circles high above Boston while Marty rearranged the cards in his pocket that listed the places he planned to explore in the next three days.

Now Boston was off the list. He turned to Eddie and asked:

"Where we go now? Explore Indian Territory? Great Plains? Detroit Factories? Oregon Northwest?"

Eddie stopped him.

"Marty, what do you say if we don't explore any more today."

Marty frowned.

"Look, Marty," said Eddie, "don't you think you ought to study that instruction book on how to fly this brand new space ship? Maybe if we tried to fly straight back to the farm, then you could spend the day studying your book and tomorrow . . ."

Marty's frown became deeper. His hand moved towards the dial of the Automatic Synchronized Pilot.

Eddie spoke faster.

"Look it, Marty, what about Earth Moisture?"

"Earth Moisture?" said Marty.

"Yes, sure, Earth Moisture. You know how it spoils your Martinean machines. You'll have to get this space ship under cover before night. You could put it in my grandmother's barn; there's lots of room. Now if you go and make a couple of more small mistakes before we start back to the farm, you might not get the space ship under cover before sunset. And then when the dew begins to fall . . ."

Marty leaned back and he thought a moment, then he nodded.

"Yes, return to farm," he said.

"Are you sure you can make the farm with one try?" asked Eddie.

"Yes, can make pinpoint landing," said Marty, firmly.

"How come you're so sure?"

"Leave small piece of Zurianomatichrome wire in sealed container under apple tree," said Marty. He reached over and pushed a button under a small transparent machine.

The little machine lit up and Eddie heard a shrill Beep Beep sound. "This beam from Secret Power Z at apple tree. Use same beam to come to Earth . . . make pinpoint landing."

Then Eddie thought of something else.

"Yeh . . . But how are we gonna get the space ship out of the apple orchard and down to the barn? A couple of small mistakes might keep us flying around all night aiming at the barn."

Marty held up one finger and smiled.

"Can do . . . watch," then he set the dial of the Automatic Synchronized Pilot and Z-i-p . . . In a few minutes the little green automobile was standing on the dirt road that ran alongside of Grandfather's apple tree where Eddie first saw it!

Marty and Eddie climbed out of the little green automobile and in another minute with the help of Marty's speed buttons they stood in Eddie's grandmother's barnyard.

"Now comes space ship," announced Marty.

He pressed a small button on his belt. And in just about a minute the little green automobile came down the dirt road from the apple orchard. It floated just a few inches above the ground. It really looked perfectly natural. As if someone had forgotten to put on the brakes and the little green automobile was rolling down the gentle slope of the dirt road.

But when the automobile came to the fence around the barnyard, it did not come into the gate as Eddie had expected it would. The little green automobile gently hopped over the fence and flopped down in the barnyard a few feet from where they stood.

The chickens and ducks screamed, squawked and quacked and rushed off in all directions like an explosion of feathers.

Eddie's grandmother looked out her kitchen window. "E-d-d-i-e," she called, "what happened?"

"Nothing, Grandma," shouted Eddie.

"What's that little automobile doing in our barnyard?"

"It's Marty's automobile, Grandma. Can he keep it in the barn a few days?"

"Of course he can, Eddie," said his grandmother. "It's a very pretty automobile, Marty . . . can you drive it? O-o-h! My chickens are burning . . ." and Eddie's grandmother rushed back to her frying chickens.

Marty walked into the barn and again pressed the little button in the center of his belt. The little green automobile floated after him and stopped right in front of him.

"Oh boy, Marty!" said Eddie, enthusiastically, "that was neat."

Marty and Eddie spent the rest of the afternoon in the barn. Eddie fussed with some things on his workbench. Marty sat on the top of his little green automobile and studied the little luminous instruction book, *How to Fly a Very Modern Martinean Interspacial Superphotic Astral Rocket Disk.*

Now and then he would grunt and nod his head as he read something that cleared up one of the things he had not understood about his space ship.

76

After a while Eddie interrupted Marty's studies to show him the Secret Power Z charged telegraph set.

Marty took his nose out of his book long enough to look at the telegraph set. He just shrugged his shoulders and said, "This natural," and went back to his book.

And when Eddie asked how Marty, way off in Martinea, knew that Eddie's telegraph set was charged with Secret Power Z, Marty answered that he did not know.

It took him sixteen Earth days traveling at maximum speed to get from Martinea to the planet Earth. And as he sped through space dodging distant suns, planets, meteors and other heavenly bodies, he occasionally sent out messages every now and then aimed at the piece of Secret Power Z Wire (the Zurianomatichrome Wire) he had buried in a sealed container in the apple orchard.

He just clicked out the message to Eddie because he had learned Morse Code from the *Boy Scout Manual* that Eddie gave him. He had not expected any answer to his message. He had been just as surprised to get a message from Eddie as Eddie was to get a message from him.

"O-h-h . . . that's it!" said Eddie. "That's why for the past two weeks the lamps and fuses kept blowing out when Grandma touched them while she was wearing that ring."

"What said?" asked Marty.

"Nothing, Marty," said Eddie, "I was just thinking out

loud. Look, Marty, this new space ship . . . Do you use Secret Power Z in this space ship too?"

Marty shook his head.

"Modern Martinean Interspacial Dychromatic Rocket Disk use newest Secret Power. Much more powerful force than Secret Power Z."

"What is it?" asked Eddie. "What do you call it? Where do you keep it?"

Marty looked at Eddie for a long minute.

He had found that Eddie was completely trustworthy and friendly last summer. He knew Eddie would not betray his secret. And Eddie knew that Marty's mission to explore the United States of America was a completely friendly and peaceful mission.

He had told Eddie last summer that the only reason he had come to the United States of America was just "scientific curiosity." The Scientists of Martinea wanted to know about the people and civilizations on the small planet Earth.

But Marty seemed uncertain now whether he should tell Eddie of this newest Secret Power.

"A-a-w . . . come on, Marty," said Eddie, "I won't tell anybody. What's your new Secret Power that is a stronger force than Secret Power Z?"

Then after another moment of silence Marty said, "Secret Power that is stronger than Secret Power Z is . . .

Secret Power Z Z Z! Zupperior Zonetic Zurianomatichrome! This third most powerful force in whole universe!"

"O-o-h Boy!" said Eddie. He was very impressed. "And where do you keep this Secret Power Z Z Z, Marty?"

Marty explained in some detail, using many scientific Martinean words that Eddie could not understand at all, that the Secret Power Z Z Z was imbedded and woven through the little green automobile!

And all the buttons on his belt and the gimmicks and gadgets that Marty carried in his pockets were automatically recharged every time he sat in the space ship.

"W-e-l-l . . . What do you know about that," said Eddie.

Marty returned to studying his book and Eddie fussed around with the things on his workbench. Suddenly he stopped working when he thought of something else he had to know.

"Hey, Marty," said Eddie, "look it here now. Since Zurianomat . . . (Eddie could not pronounce that word Zurianomatichrome).

"Zurianomatichrome?" said Marty as easily as if he were just saying mush.

"Yeh, that . . . since you said last summer that it could not stand Earth Moisture, what if it rains while you're out exploring the United States? It won't be as easy to put this green automobile under cover as it was the Secret Power Z Wire."

"Will no rain," said Marty firmly.

"But Marty, how can you be so sure?"

"Martinean Meteorological Scientists prepare Weather Forecast for Earth." Marty took another of those cards out of his pocket and he read, "Forecast for United States of America, Earth . . . Fair, Sunny, Hot . . . No Precipitation . . . 1 day 7 month . . . to . . . 5 day 7 month. Martinean Meteorological Scientist never make mistake."

But Eddie was a little doubtful. He knew that Meteorological Scientist meant weather man and Precipitation meant rain.

"Well, I hope they're right," said Eddie.

And again there was silence for a few minutes in the barn until Marty snapped his little luminous book shut and hopped off the top of the automobile where he had been sitting.

"Now understand Modern Martinean Interspacial Superphotic Astral Rocket Disk," he said, triumphantly. "Now go explore Indian Territory . . . Great Plains . . . Oregon Northwest . . ."

"*Now*, Marty?" exclaimed Eddie. "*Now?* . . . Before supper?"

Marty frowned.

"Look it, Marty, here's something I wanted to ask you all day," said Eddie. "Is that thing . . . that map up over your instrument board supposed to be a map of the United States?"

Marty brought out his Autotranslation Dictionary Box and said, "Map."

The face of the box lit up . . . Martinean words flashed across its surface and he read:

"Map . . . Geographical Chart."

Then he looked at Eddie and said, "Yes. This Geographical Chart. This map of United States of America."

Eddie slowly shook his head.

"M-m-m, I dunno about that, Marty," he said. "Now I believe you when you tell me the Martinean Scientists never make mistakes. But whoever drew that map . . . What do they call those Scientists? Geog . . . Geographers or something. Well . . . that map's wrong! And maybe if you have been flying by that map, it's no wonder you made a couple of small mistakes today."

"No Martinean Scientist draw map," Marty confessed. "I draw map from your geography book."

"O-oh," said Eddie, "so you drew it. Well, it's pretty good for someone who . . . Look, Marty, what do you say we draw that map over again right now. I got some good airline company maps. We can copy them and then tomorrow . . ."

Eddie pulled out some folded maps from a drawer in

his workbench. He spread them out for Marty to see. They were good maps. And it was just then while they were looking over the maps that Eddie noticed for the first time Marty did not wear a Merit Badge for "Surveying and Map Making."

At last Marty nodded.

"Yes," he said, "you draw map."

And he and Eddie put on their visualizers and climbed into the space ship. Before Eddie's grandmother called them in for supper they had wiped out Marty's map on the illuminated panel over the instrument board and Eddie drew a proper map of the United States.

It had only a few small mistakes.

CHAPTER EIGHT

Chief Tommy Longbow

THERE were many difficulties to be overcome next morning before Marty could get his space ship out of the barn and continue his exploration of the United States of America.

First of all there were the chickens!

They had roosted all night on the space ship and they liked its smooth surface so much they would not leave! The biggest and fattest hens particularly liked sitting on the invisible part of the space ship. Perhaps it made them feel that they were floating or gliding in the air like graceful little birds, which they were not!

Marty and Eddie shooed them off again and again but they kept coming back. And they stubbornly would not get out of the way so that Marty could get his space ship out of the barn and into the yard where he could blast off.

And then there was the weather!

A few tiny fluffy clouds appeared in the sky. And in spite of Marty's faith in the weather forecast made by the Meteorologists (weather men) on Martinea that rain would not fall in the United States during the four days of his visit, Marty was worried.

He walked back and forth, back and forth, in the barnyard angrily watching those innocent little clouds until they lazily floated across the heavens and disappeared over the horizon.

Eddie patrolled the barnyard with him. He knew what a little Earth Moisture could do to a Martinean machine. The space ship, by just passing through one of those innocent (but damp) little clouds, might fall apart at once and he and Marty would go crashing down.

And then there was Eddie's grandmother!

After breakfast she insisted on coming down to the barn to watch them drive away . . . "to go off exploring in Marty's pretty little green automobile," as she said.

Eddie had all he could do to keep her from trying to open the door of the little green automobile just to feel the upholstery on the seats.

He finally pulled a loose button off his Scout shirt and asked his grandmother to sew it on again. And while he went back to the house with her to get her sewing basket, Marty managed in spite of the chickens underfoot to get the space ship out of the barn.

It seemed all the chickens did not get safely out of his way because one fat hen limped around the barnyard as if some heavy object had passed over one of her toes.

There were a lot of loose feathers still floating in the air when Eddie raced back to the barnyard leaving his grandmother to put away her sewing basket.

The moment Eddie got to the yard, Marty and he climbed into the space ship and Z-i-p . . . they were off!

"Where we going?" asked Eddie as Marty pushed and twisted a gadget here and a button there.

"Washington, D.C.," said Marty promptly.

"Aw . . . Marty!" said Eddie, "let's not start that again! Let's not try to fly to Washington until you're sure you know how to fly this space ship right. Let's take one practice flight . . . Just one before we go to Washington. Where'll we go?"

Marty stopped his button pushing and gadget twisting to pick off a few chicken feathers that still clung to his clothes. He twirled a feather slowly as he thought.

"Explore Indian Territory . . . Great Plains?" he suggested.

"That's a good idea," said Eddie. "Let's go."

"Where is Indians?" asked Marty.

"Indians?" repeated Eddie. "Oh, there are Indians in lots of places."

He moved his finger around the map he had drawn up over the instrument panel.

"Look, there's Indians here up in Martha's Vineyard and there's Indians here down in the Carolinas and there's Indians further down south about here," Eddie's finger skipped across the Seminole Indians in Florida without mentioning them to go west to "here in Mexico . . . and out here in California . . ."

Marty nodded. Then he reached forward and picked the most distant spot Eddie had pointed to.

"Go here," he said.

"But why go way out there?" asked Eddie.

Marty explained that in studying his instruction book on how to fly his new space ship yesterday he learned it was easier to fly long distances than short distances . . . for beginners.

Then Marty twisted the dial of the Automatic Synchronized Pilot and set the long needle so that it pointed to the distant spot he had picked on the chart.

The space ship stopped circling and shot off in a great swooping arc up through the dark blue sky of the iconosphere.

In a very short time Marty shouted, "Hold breath for dive!"

And just about the instant Eddie shut his mouth, Marty reached forward and pushed the button that held the space ship in mid-air. Then the space ship flew in wide circles while Marty looked down through his small, powerful telescope for a spot to land.

Suddenly he pushed another button. The space ship hovered in one spot. Marty took another look through his telescope and quickly passed it to Eddie with a proud smile.

"Look," he said.

Eddie peeked into the powerful little telescope. He found that he was looking at an Indian village! There were feathered Braves! . . . Squaws! . . . Papooses! . . . Horses! . . . Wigwams . . .

"Indians!" he cried, "Marty, you hit it right on the nose!"

"Hold breath for landing," shouted Marty.

In another instant the space ship landed gently right in back of the biggest wigwam in the Indian village.

Their swift landing went unnoticed. Marty and Eddie climbed out of the space ship which now of course looked like a little green automobile and they walked around to the front of the wigwam.

A tall, bronzed half-naked Indian brave stood there with

his arms folded across his chest. There were feathers dangling from his long, black, braided hair and streaks of paint marked his bony face.

Marty and Eddie stood looking up at the Indian but he stared off into space and paid no attention to them.

Marty whispered out of the side of his mouth to Eddie: "How you speak to American Indians?"

"I dunno," whispered Eddie, "you can begin by saying . . . 'How' . . . I think."

Marty stepped around in front of the tall Indian.

"How," he said in a loud voice.

The Indian looked down at Marty.

"How . . . what?" asked the Indian.

His jaws began to move slowly. Eddie thought the Indian looked as if he were chewing gum.

"How are you?" said Marty.

The tall Indian unfolded his arms, stared down at Marty, then at Eddie. He really was chewing gum! Then he looked up and shouted:

"HEY! . . . WHAT GOES ON HERE . . . WHO LET THESE KIDS ON THE LOT?"

People came running from all directions . . . Indians, cowboys, and other people dressed in ordinary clothes!

"What's going on here?" shouted an important looking man wearing a cap and carrying a batch of typewritten sheets of paper in his hand. "What's the matter? . . . How did that troop of Boy Scouts get in here? . . . How can I direct a picture if every Tom, Dick and Harry of a Boy Scout comes in and bothers my Indians? . . . No wonder the moving picture business here in Hollywood is falling apart! Any Tom, Dick or Harry comes in on the lot . . ."

Then he interrupted himself.

"Hey!" he screamed to some men half-hidden by a clump of trees, "STOP THOSE CAMERAS . . ."

Then he threw the handful of papers he carried up in the air.

"What's the use?" he groaned, "what's the use . . . Somebody get me a chair . . ."

So many people were running every which way and so many others were gathered around the important stout man with the cap, no one noticed Marty and Eddie.

They joined the crowd around the stout man. Then they wandered off and explored the Indian village. Eddie explained to Marty about wampum, tomahawks, and everything else he knew about Indian lore.

They looked into the wigwams. And when they peeked under the door flap of the biggest wigwam . . . the one near the spot where they landed the space ship, they saw an old Indian sitting there with his old squaw playing casino on a big Indian drum.

They were sitting on the floor of the wigwam cross-legged on a couple of buffalo robes. The old Indian wore a big feathered war bonnet and the squaw wore glasses.

"Come in, boys, come in," said the old Indian. "Don't stand there in the door. Come in and sit on these genuine buffalo robes."

Eddie and Marty sat down cross-legged.

"What's your name, son?"

"My name's Eddie and he's my friend, Marty."

"Eddie and Marty, eh . . . Are you in the big scene too?" asked the old Indian. "I didn't know they were using Boy Scouts in the big battle scene."

"No sir," said Eddie, and he shook his head.

"So you're not actors, eh?" said the old Indian.

"We explorers," said Marty to Eddie's surprise.

"Explorers, eh," the old Indian chuckled, "so you're explorers . . . not actors . . . well, I'll tell you the truth," and the old Indian leaned towards them and whispered hoarsely, "neither am I. I'm not an actor either. I'm Chief Tommy Longbow and this is my wife, Mrs. Little Deer Longbow . . ."

"Are you really an Indian . . . I mean an Indian chief?" asked Eddie.

"Yes sir, I sure am . . . as sure as I'm sitting here. I'm Chief of all those Indians out there all painted up like a lot of savages . . ."

And Chief Tommy Longbow slapped his knee and laughed so hard he almost fell over backward.

His laugh was so hearty Mrs. Longbow, Eddie, and even Marty smiled.

"Well, how come you're here if you're not an actor?" asked Eddie when Chief Tommy Longbow quieted down.

"Now I'll tell you, son, Mrs. Longbow here and I own a few oil wells and a few thousand acres of good land out in Colorado. Every now and then some of these Hollywood picture fellows come out our way looking for real Indians. Whenever that happens and Mrs. Longbow and I think we ought to have a vacation we get into our Cadillac station wagon and pile in a lot of my sons and grandsons and their wives and kids and we pick up a couple of more dozen members of the tribe with their cars. We come and have us a real fine vacation out here . . . camping out, living on the fat of the land. And we get paid for it! Can you imagine that? We get paid for it!"

Chief Tommy Longbow went off again into such a gale of laughter that tears came to his eyes. After he regained control of himself and wiped away the tears with a large bandanna handkerchief he said:

"So you boys are explorers. What you exploring?"

"United States of America," said Marty.

"Just parts of the United States," said Eddie, quickly.

"Where you come from?" asked Chief Tommy Longbow.

"New York State," said Eddie before Marty could answer. "We're just exploring around."

"New York, eh? . . . And where you bound for?"

"Well, . . . huh . . . we expect . . . we hope to go back by way of Washington, D.C.," said Eddie.

And Marty nodded.

"Going back by way of Washington, D.C., eh? Say, you boys got a lot of spunk. I've known a lot of fellows went to Washington but they were a lot older men than you are. Yes, I've known a few Presidents . . . the Great White Fathers."

"You've known some Presidents of the United States!" exclaimed Eddie.

"Yes, I've known some . . . They come through Colorado when they were running for the Presidency and many a time I got myself dressed up in this Indian uniform of mine with my beads and all my feathers and I'd put a big feathered war bonnet on some presidential candidate's head. That would make him an honorary chief of the Chuckawaga Tribe . . . that's my tribe, son. There'd be photographers all over the place. Yes sir, some of those men became the Presidents of this here United States. Some didn't, but they got their war bonnets anyway."

Eddie and Marty were so impressed they couldn't say a thing for a few minutes.

Then Eddie blurted out something that had been worrying him for a few days.

"Chief Longbow," began Eddie.

"Chief Tommy Longbow, boy," said the Chief.

"Chief Tommy Longbow . . . I've been wondering about something. Maybe since you know Presidents who went to Washington you could tell me. When explorers come from someplace . . . to explore some other place, do they need . . . do they always carry passports and visiting permits and things like that?"

Chief Tommy Longbow knit his brows and thought for a moment.

"I don't know, Eddie, seems to me when Christopher Columbus and the other explorers came from Europe, we Indians didn't ask them if they had a passport or a visiting permit. No sir, they just came. How come you're asking a question like that, son?"

"I was just thinking," said Eddie, "I was just thinking say . . . well, just for an example, say if a Space Man explorer were to some day come from another planet, do you think he'd have to have a passport or something to visit Washington, the capital of the United States?"

"That's a pretty big if . . . you said there, Eddie," said Chief Tommy Longbow. "If a Space Man explorer came to Washington, but mind you, I'm not saying that's impossible. Mrs. Longbow's great-great-grandfather told a story of once meeting a little man out in the desert, he had dropped out of the sky riding on a big silver bird . . . yes

sir, and he said they smoked a peace pipe together. Isn't that so, Little Deer?"

Mrs. Longbow smiled brightly and nodded her head.

"Well, the way I see it," continued Chief Tommy Longbow, "we have no way yet of giving visiting permits or providing passports to anybody out there in space. I think if a peaceful Space Man explorer were to go visit Washington, he wouldn't need a passport or a visiting permit. I think they'd be glad to see him."

Right after Chief Tommy Longbow had answered Eddie's question Marty stood up.

"Maybe we go now," he said to Eddie.

Eddie stood up too.

"Yeh . . . Well, . . . Thanks a lot," said Eddie.

"Just a second. Now don't go running off. If you two

explorers are going on to Washington I think I got something for you." Chief Tommy Longbow laboriously got to his feet and walked over to the side of the wigwam to a buckskin bag that hung there. He reached into the bag and pulled out a number of feathered bonnets. He picked out two of them and brought them over to Eddie and Marty.

"I always carry a few spare war bonnets," he said, "and when I meet some worthy men I make them honorary chiefs of the Chuckawaga Tribe. Hold your head still, son," he said to Eddie as he put a war bonnet on Eddie's head. "Now you, boy," and he put the other war bonnet on Marty's head. Marty's war bonnet was a little too big for him and rested on his ears.

"There you are," said Chief Tommy Longbow, "you boys are now honorary Chiefs of the Chuckawaga Tribe . . . Blood Brothers of the Great Braves of the Colorado Deserts. When you get to Washington you tell them that. It will open doors for you."

Then Chief Tommy Longbow shook them both by the hand. And just about the time he completed that impressive ceremony there was a great shouting outside the wigwam.

"Places . . . Places everybody! . . . We're going to shoot the big battle scene."

"That's our cue," said the old Chief and he helped Mrs. Longbow get to her feet.

And as Eddie and Marty were thanking Chief Tommy Longbow and Mrs. Little Deer Longbow and saying good-bye, someone outside shouted again:

"Throw some bushes over that little green automobile behind the big wigwam. It's in the range of the cameras."

"That's ours," cried Eddie, as he and Marty rushed out of the wigwam.

And whoever it was that was sent to throw bushes over that little green automobile never found it. It was just as if the little green automobile had disappeared into thin air.

CHAPTER NINE

Marty's War Bonnet

IF it had not been for that Indian war bonnet that Chief Tommy Longbow gave Marty, his space ship might well have landed in Washington, D.C. that very day!

The war bonnet was a little too large for Marty and it kept slipping down over his eyes. But Marty would wear it even though he could hardly see the gadgets and buttons on his instrument panel.

And then as he leaned forward to set the Automatic Synchronized Pilot for Washington, D.C. the very moment the space ship left Hollywood, California, the big war bonnet slipped down over his face and engulfed his head right down to his shoulders!

And since he blindly twisted the dial that set their destination, by the time Marty could, with Eddie's help, work the big war bonnet back above his eyes, the space ship was aimed straight at New Orleans!

Marty just had time to shout, "Hold breath for landing!" . . . and they were there!

Fortunately, the space ship landed in a palm-fringed little park.

New Orleans was not on Marty's list of cities or places to be explored. But since they were there he and Eddie whirled through the streets at top speed. Eddie had lost his own Indian war bonnet in the mad rush out of Chief Tommy Longbow's wigwam. He offered to hold Marty's war bonnet but Marty would have none of that.

Now Marty dressed in his strange Boy Scout uniform with its too many pockets and that rash of Merit Badges and studded belt and topped by the oversized feathered war bonnet, did look a little peculiar.

But the people of New Orleans who saw him flash by along the streets paid no undue attention to his unusual appearance.

They may have thought Marty was something left over from last spring's Mardi Gras when everybody in New Orleans dresses up in fantastic costumes and cavorts through the streets.

Leaving New Orleans and again headed for Washington, Marty tried to avoid flying through a lonely cloud that crossed their path when the space ship blasted off. As a result and because his big war bonnet slipped, the space ship splashed down to a clumsy landing in the stockyards of Chicago!

Marty was so angry at the cloud, the clumsy landing and the discovery that he had again made a small thousand mile mistake, he roared his space ship out of Chicago without even looking at the city . . .. although it was on his list.

And at last on the third try Marty almost landed his space ship in Washington, D.C.! He missed Washington by only a little more than a hundred miles! (a hundred and thirty-seven miles, to be exact). He landed his space ship in

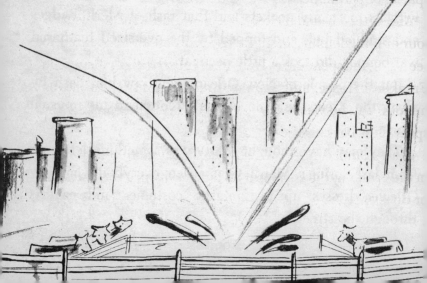

Philadelphia! And Marty was elated!

"Now," he said to Eddie, "now can almost control Interpacial Superphotic Astral Rocket Disk!"

And after he and Eddie had made an almost leisurely tour of Philadelphia, he saw and recorded all he wanted to see . . . Independence Hall, the Liberty Bell, Benjamin Franklin's House, and a number of museums, all in eleven minutes flat, he was ready to call it a day. Then he flew the space ship back to the farm.

Marty landed his space ship so neatly and gently right in the center of the barnyard he did not disturb the chickens or ducks at all.

"How come you made the barnyard in one try?" asked Eddie as they climbed out of the space ship.

Marty explained he had found that Secret Power Z wire ring that he had given Eddie's grandmother last summer on Eddie's workbench. And he placed it in a sealed container and buried it in the center of the barnyard. Now he could, at will, make a pinpoint landing either in the orchard or in the barnyard. He could come flying in on the beam from the Secret Power Z.

He said he had just borrowed the ring and would give it back to Eddie's grandmother when he blasted off for Martinea again.

"Don't!" said Eddie. "Look, Marty, it's a very pretty ring and Grandma appreciates it. But when she wears it and turns on electric lights, that ring blows the fuses . . ."

Marty snorted and shook his head. He disagreed with Eddie's unscientific reasoning. But then he nodded.

"Yes, I give grandmother other ring."

"Oh . . . maybe we'd better buy one," said Eddie quickly. He had a vague image of Marty giving his grandmother a ring made of Secret Power Z Z Z . . . the third most powerful force in the universe. Such a ring would not only blow the fuses on Eddie's grandmother's farm, it might ruin the electric works of the whole Hudson River Valley!

"Tell you what, Marty, when we go exploring again, we'll

buy a ring. I've got some money. Then you can give it to Grandma as a present. All right?"

"All right," said Marty.

They settled down in the barnyard to eat the big lunch Eddie's grandmother had packed in his knapsack.

As Eddie chewed on a drumstick and a sandwich, he tried to figure out how far they had traveled since 10 o'clock that morning when they left the barnyard.

He was good at mental arithmetic and when he had added up to almost ten thousand in his head, his grand-mother came into the barnyard.

She had seen them from her back porch and she came down from the house with a pitcher of milk and glasses.

"Hello," she said. "Marty, where did you get that hand-some Indian hat?"

And before Marty could say anything she went on, "You boys are back early. You couldn't have gone very far. Here, hold these glasses and I'll pour you some milk. It's only 12 o'clock. What happened? Did your little automobile run out of gasoline?"

Eddie's and Marty's mouths were so full of fried chicken and cucumber sandwiches they could not have answered if they'd wanted to.

"Eddie, did you pass Washington's Rock while you were exploring?" asked his grandmother.

Eddie shook his head.

"That's too bad. I got a telephone call from Mr. Pearson this morning. You remember Mr. Pearson, Marty, the Scoutmaster of our village Boy Scouts. You met him last summer . . ."

Marty nodded.

"Well, Mr. Pearson telephoned and asked for you, Eddie . . . guess he didn't know Marty was here. He said the whole village is turning out for our Fourth of July celebration and the village Boy Scouts are all pitching in. And Mr. Marvel is going to string pretty red, white and blue electric lights all over it. Mr. Marvel is our village electrician, Marty . . . an awful nice man. He drives the village taxi too. Now where was I?"

Eddie's grandmother tapped her forehead.

"Yes, now I remember, well, Mr. Marvel said to Mr. Pearson and that's why he telephoned . . . Mr. Marvel said he'd rather have you, Eddie Blow, help him wire and fix all the electric lights on that bandstand than any grown man in the village. How do you like that?"

Eddie's grandmother looked proudly down at Eddie.

"That's why I asked if you drove past Washington's Rock. They're all out there now and I told Mr. Pearson to watch for you, you might be driving by. Marty, I hope you come to our Fourth of July celebration. We have the nicest Fourth of July celebration of any village or town in this part of the state, don't we, Eddie?"

"You're right, Grandma," said Eddie. "It's really true, Marty. There are fireworks and everything."

"There now, Marty, Eddie says so and he's from New York City! Yes, we always have the village band playing and we have speeches and lemonade and then there's the most beautiful fireworks display you ever saw. We have rockets and pinwheels and it ends with the prettiest picture in fireworks. Mind you, Marty, a breathing image of George Washington right up there on Washington's Rock. Sometimes we only have a great big blazing American flag but this year we're going to have the best ever. We're going to have pictures of George Washington, Abraham Lincoln and our newly elected village mayor, Mr. Sills. I guess he's paying for the gunpowder for his own picture and above them all a great big American flag."

Eddie's grandmother poured herself a glass of milk and drank it and then she went on.

"Mr. Marvel is building the wooden frames for the fireworks that make those pictures up on Washington's Rock, too. The Boy Scouts are helping. But he especially asked for you, Eddie. And you can help too if you want to, Marty."

Eddie looked at Marty. Marty was thinking. At last he nodded his head.

"That's fine. I'm sure Mr. Pearson and Mr. Marvel will appreciate your help, Marty. Now do be careful when you go up there, boys, climbing around on Washington's Rock."

CHAPTER TEN

Danger — Explosives

"Hya, Eddie! Hya Boy! Who's the Indian Chief? It's Marty! Hya, Marty. Hya, Boy!"

Eddie and Marty were greeted with so much warmth and enthusiasm by the village Boy Scouts when they got to Washington's Rock they were very glad that they came. But Eddie wished Marty had not insisted on wearing his Indian war bonnet.

There were Boy Scouts climbing, clinging, and crawling all over the place.

They were climbing trees, clinging to the bare face of the cliff called Washington's Rock and crawling all over the top of it and on the broad meadow in front of it. They were sawing and hammering away on a bandstand and stringing and stretching bunting and wires through the trees under the supervision of Mr. Marvel. And racing this way and that shouting orders and blowing his whistle was the village Scoutmaster, Mr. Pearson.

He carried a large pad of paper and a bunch of pencils in one hand and his whistle in the other.

Mr. Pearson ran over to Eddie and Marty.

"Hello, Scouts. Hello, Scouts. We need every hand. Lots to do . . . lots to do . . . Oh, it's you, Eddie. Good man . . . and . . . and . . . ?" Mr. Pearson bent down and peeked under Marty's big Indian war bonnet and asked, "And who?"

"I Marty," said Marty.

"Marty? Oh, yes, yes, yes," said Mr. Pearson, "Marty . . . Of course, the Cub Scout who raced off with so many ribbons last summer . . ."

(Marty had, with a little help from Secret Power Z, won most of the races at last summer's Scout Jamboree.)

"Good man . . . Good man," cried Mr. Pearson, and he straightened up and shouted, "Oh! Mr. Marvel. Mr. Marvel, I've got two more good men for you . . . Eddie Blow and Marty. Eddie, you go right over and dig into it with Mr. Marvel. He asked especially for you . . . You're his right-hand man. And you, Marty, well, you go along with Eddie. There's lots to do . . . there's lots to do."

And Mr. Pearson ran off scribbling on his large pad and blowing his whistle.

Mr. Marvel was a thin, slow-moving, soft-spoken man.

"H'llo, Eddie," he said when Eddie and Marty found him. "Need you bad around here. Need a man who knows electricity."

He pointed out the work he wanted Eddie to tackle. There were some electric wires to be strung around the poles of the bandstand. Then after a long look at Marty he said, "You come along with me, Big Chief."

And Mr. Marvel walked slowly up the steep path that led to the top of Washington's Rock.

There were a crew of Scouts on the flat top of the rock noisily hammering away on some large wooden frames.

"That's enough, Scouts," he said. "Thanks."

He swung one of the hammers once or twice on the crooked and protruding nails of the frame, then he turned to Marty and said, "Follow me, Big Chief."

He led Marty over to a big packing case marked "Danger —Explosives."

Mr. Marvel unlocked the case and motioned for Marty to look into it. He pointed to six black squat kegs.

"That's gunpowder, Big Chief. If you see anybody lighting matches, stop them. If you can't stop them, run."

Marty nodded.

Then Mr. Marvel picked two rolls of heavy wire, a smaller roll of thin wire and two pairs of pliers out of the case. He hung a roll of wire on Marty's shoulder and handed him a pair of pliers. And he picked up the other wire, the pliers, locked the case and walked back to the wood frame. Marty followed.

"Here's what we're doing on this frame, Big Chief," said Mr. Marvel. He took a small sheet of paper out of the breast pocket of his shirt and unfolded it for Marty to see.

"Looks like him, don't it?" he said.

It was a crude pencil outline drawing of George Washington copied from a picture on a one dollar bill.

"Looks like who?" asked Marty.

"George Washington," said Mr. Marvel.

"Yes. Look like him," said Marty.

"Pull that war bonnet up off your eyes, Big Chief, you'll see better," said Mr. Marvel.

After Mr. Marvel made some marks on the wood frame with a thick black crayon he cut off a long section of the heavy wire with his pliers. Then he lashed one end of the wire to the wood frame with a piece of thinner wire. He bent the heavy wire in big curves with his pliers again and lashed another section of it to the frame.

He pointed out spots where he wanted Marty to twist small wire around the heavy wire. Although he worked quickly Marty kept up with him. In a little while Mr. Marvel stood up and rubbed his back.

"You're a good worker, Big Chief," he said. "Well, there he is, old George Washington himself."

Marty looked at the bent wire lashed to the wood frame. He nodded. He too could see that with his help Mr. Marvel had made a large outline drawing of George Washington in heavy wire and lashed it to the wood frame.

And as soon as the other frames were ready Mr. Marvel and Marty finished them off lickety-split. They put a wire drawing of Abraham Lincoln on one, Mr. Sills, mayor of the village, on another and the flag of the United States of America on the last frame. Mr. Marvel had made his pencil drawing of Mayor Sills from an old campaign poster. But the flag of the United States he had drawn from memory . . . right out of his own head.

As the afternoon wore on some of the grownups from the village, Captain Jack, the grocer, and some ladies and Mayor Sills himself came around, but they did not do any work. They just stood around and watched and talked with Mr. Pearson.

Mayor Sills walked around saying encouraging words to all the working Scouts. He was a big heavy man and when he climbed up the very steep path that led to the top of Washington's Rock, he stopped halfway and took a little rest as he struck a match to light a big cigar.

Like a flash Marty hopped off the frame where he was working and rushed down the path.

"No light match," he said, sternly.

"What . . . What was that?" exclaimed Mayor Sills still holding his lit match.

Eddie ran up the path from the meadow and Mr. Marvel looked over the edge of Washington's Rock and called down to the Mayor.

"We got gunpowder up here, Mr. Mayor."

"Gunpowder! You're right, my boy, glad you told me. Can't take a chance with fire in this dry weather," and the Mayor shook his match out and continued his climb up the path.

Everybody settled down to work again. Mr. Marvel and Marty next carried a large roll of paper and the six black squat kegs of gunpowder from the big packing case over to the big wire pictures they had made.

Mr. Marvel opened the kegs. He told Marty that the gunpowder in each keg burnt with a different color. One burned red, one white, one blue, one green, one purple and one orange.

He unrolled the paper and then scooped up some gunpowder from one keg and sprinkled it in a little straight pile along the center of that paper. Then he and Marty made long paper-wrapped, gunpowder-filled sausages and tied them to all the thick wires they had lashed to the frames.

When all the paper sausages were tied on in place, Marty helped Mr. Marvel carry the half empty powder kegs back to the case marked "Danger—Explosives." One keg had developed a leak . . . the keg with the red burning gunpowder . . . and Mr. Marvel saw the little ridge of gunpowder that it had dropped stretch from the wood frames to the case.

"That's dangerous, Big Chief," he said and he and Marty kicked the gunpowder around and tried to bury it in the dirt.

"Guess that will be all right, Big Chief. Anyway, I'll be

the only one up here when I light the fireworks and I'll watch out."

As the afternoon ended almost everything was done.

The bandstand was finished. The bunting was hung, the electric wires strung and the colored bulbs screwed into their sockets down in the meadow in front of Washington's Rock. And the four big firework pictures lashed to the big wood frames were erected on the top of the rock.

Mr. Pearson who could make a speech at the drop of a hat dropped his hat as he mopped his forehead and made a speech.

"That's it for the day, Scouts," he said. "You've done a fine day's work. Tomorrow we're going to have the biggest bang up Fourth of July ever seen in these parts. Now there are just a few more things. Everybody who can, please come back here tomorrow morning. There's still a lot to do . . . a lot to do. And I expect you all will be ushers at night and you will serve the lemonade. Remember I said serve it . . . not swallow it."

And after that joke Mr. Pearson said, "Dismissed," and everybody went home to supper.

Eddie and Marty were the first ones home (of course). But it took a little extra time to get back to the farm because the Boy Scouts from the village fooled around.

They joshed Marty a little about his Merit Badges and a

lot about his oversized Indian war bonnet. When they asked him where he got it, he said simply, "From Indian Chief Tommy Longbow."

"From Indian Chief Tommy Longbow?" exclaimed one village Boy Scout. "What kind of an Indian Chief is he? . . . an Indian rubber chief?"

"No," said Marty, "real Indian Chief. Chief of Chuckawaga Tribe. I honorary Chief of Chuckawaga Tribe . . . Blood Brothers to the Braves of the Colorado Desert."

"WHAT!" exclaimed all the village Boy Scouts together. "You're an honorary Chief of the . . . What's this kid talking about, Eddie? . . ."

"He's right . . . It's true," said Eddie, sincerely. "He really is an Honorary Chief . . . like he said."

The whole troop of village Boy Scouts stopped right there in the road . . . their mouths hung open and their eyes popped!

Eddie and Marty walked quietly on and turned into the road to Eddie's grandmother's farm and the village Boy Scouts silently looked after them.

CHAPTER ELEVEN

The Hero of Washington's Rock

"W-H-O-O-P! . . . W-H-O-O-P! . . . W-H-O-O-P! . . . W-H-O-O-P!"

They had hardly sat down to supper when they heard a repeated unearthly howl of a distant siren . . .

Eddie's grandmother jumped to her feet.

"There's a fire somewhere," she cried. "Hear that siren, Eddie, that's our new village fire siren. You can hear it for fifteen miles. Dear me, there's a fire somewhere. Did you count those siren shrieks, Eddie?"

At that moment the siren howled again.

"W-H-O-O-P! . . . W-H-O-O-P! . . . W-H-O-O-P! . . . W-H-O-O-P!"

"There were four signals, Grandma," said Eddie.

"Let me see . . . Four? . . . Four? . . . Why, signal four is . . . There's a fire near Washington's Rock!"

115

"Washington's Rock! The fireworks!" exclaimed Eddie and Marty all in one breath.

They jumped to their feet and started for the door.

"Eddie . . . Marty!" cried Eddie's grandmother, "where are you going?"

"We'll be right back, Grandma," shouted Eddie as he and Marty ran out through the back door.

"Be careful, Eddie. Do be careful . . ."

But neither Eddie or Marty heard what she said. They were already around the last curve on the road to Washington's Rock.

The fire at Washington's Rock had a good start before Eddie and Marty got there. The brush and young trees on the side of the steep path up to the top of the Rock were blazing away merrily.

Eddie found some empty burlap bags that had contained some of Mr. Marvel's material and he ran and dipped them in a muddy little brook that ran across the meadow.

"Here, Marty, take one of these wet bags and start beating out that fire," shouted Eddie.

Marty held the wet bag with his fingertips and stood watching while Eddie beat the burning bushes with his wet burlap bag.

"Fire start with match Mayor dropped," he said.

Eddie stopped beating the fire and turned around. His face was flushed from the heat of the flames.

"WHAT!" he cried.

"Fire start with match Mayor dropped."

"Yes, sure I figured that out already," Eddie said, impatiently, "but we gotta beat it out. Use that wet bag."

"Very unscientific method," said Marty.

By that time, with roaring engines and clanging bells, the Village Volunteer Firemen arrived. They rushed their hoses across the meadow and pulled a small gasoline motor pump into place. The Mayor, Mr. Pearson, Captain Jack, and a lot of other men and all the village Boy Scouts came running.

Everybody had burlap bags. And they climbed over each other to dip the bags into the little muddy brook. The Volunteer Firemen threw a hose into the brook and started their gasoline motor pump chugging along. Some firemen held the hose pointing at the blazing bushes and trees . . . and they waited for the water to come gushing out of the nozzle of their hose.

The gasoline motor pumped and pumped . . . and chugged and chugged . . . but no water came gushing

out! At last a sluggish trickle of very muddy water dripped
out of the hose and splashed on the ground!

So many burlap bags had been dipped in that little muddy
brook . . . only half of them getting wet . . . the little
muddy brook just dried up!

Everybody started beating the bushes but the fire
crackled merrily along. And the flames started to creep
slowly up the side of the cliff!

They were fighting a losing battle until Marty worked
his way through the lines of fire fighters and he stood in
the front ranks.

He had slipped a little cylindrical object out of one of
his pockets and he deliberately pointed it at the fire!

In an instant the fire was out!

No one saw him do that except Eddie! He was up in the front ranks of the fire fighters too and as he beat the fire with his face turned from the heat of the flames, he saw his friend Marty by his side. When Marty did what he did, Eddie whispered, "Atta boy, Marty."

Marty smiled.

The Volunteer Firemen and the Boy Scouts and everyone else heaved a great sigh of relief.

"If that fire had gone just six foot further up that path," said Mr. Marvel, quietly, "you'd have seen the biggest, loudest firework display you ever saw."

Everyone nodded their heads and everyone congratulated everyone else on a job well done.

Then just as the Volunteer Firemen were rolling up their hose and everybody was getting ready to go back to eat their interrupted supper some Scout shouted:

"HEY! . . . LOOK ON TOP OF THE ROCK!"

All heads turned and looked with one motion.

Up above the clouds of smoke on the top of Washington's Rock there was a quick flash of red flame!

Some smoldering sparks must have floated up to the top of the Rock. And there they found that little spill of red gunpowder that had trickled out of the leaky keg.

The red flame ran in two directions . . . towards the big frames holding the firework pictures of George Washington, Abraham Lincoln, Mayor Sills and the American flag . . . and towards the big packing case marked "Danger—Explosives!"

There was a jamming rush as everyone at once tried to scramble up the narrow steep path that led to the top of the Rock.

But Marty held himself aloof. He calmly and quietly, under the cover of smoke that surrounded everything, pressed one of his buttons and presto, he was on the top of Washington's Rock!

No one knew how he got there (except Eddie, of course) but they could all see him dancing this way and that with his big war bonnet flopping all over his head. He looked as if he was stamping the fire out with his feet but he really was just killing that outburst of red flame promptly and effectively with his mysterious little cylinder.

A great roaring cheer went up from all the fire fighters: "'RAY . . . MARTY! . . . 'RAY . . . MARTY! . . . 'RAY . . . MARTY BOY!"

Everybody ran up the steep path to the top of Washington's Rock. Everyone except Mayor Sills. He walked. And when he came to the burned out spot alongside the path where he had lit the match he hurried by.

On top of the Rock Mayor Sills moved directly into the center of the large joyful group surrounding Marty and he raised his arms high above his head.

"Quiet please," shouted Mayor Sills. "Give me some room, my friends. There's something I want to say to this brave lad."

And after everyone had quieted down and moved back a little, Mayor Sills faced Marty and made a speech.

"Young man," he began. Then he turned from side to side and whispered, "What's his name?"

"Marty," said Eddie, who stood by Marty's side.

"Thank you, son," said the Mayor, and he began his speech again. "Marty . . . Honored guest . . . My friends and good neighbors . . . Tonight we here in the proud village of Schuyler's Landing have witnessed an event for which we all can be doubly proud. We have been privileged to witness one of the most heroic acts of self-sacrifice and bravery anyone has ever seen . . . no matter where . . . From the rock-ribbed coast of Maine to the sun-swept shores of California . . .

"My friends, the world may soon forget what I say here, but it will never forget what he did here."

The Mayor had a coughing spell and he coughed and coughed and coughed until he could think of what else to say.

Mayor Sill's son, who was one of the village Boy Scouts, whispered to his father, "Pop, Marty's a real honorary Indian Chief, a Chuckawaga Chief, honest, Eddie said so."

122

Then the Mayor resumed his speech.

"My friends, there's little we can do to repay this gallant lad who has so bravely served us all. But I hear on very good authority that he has been honored by many. I hear from an undisputable source that he has been made an Honorary Chief of the Great Chuckawaga Tribe. Can we do any less?

"I propose to call a special meeting of the village Trustees tomorrow morning. And at that meeting I shall suggest that this boy . . . this brave lad . . . Marty . . . be voted an Honorary Citizen of the village of Schuyler's Landing."

Wild shouts of approval and applause interrupted the Mayor. He held his hand high above his head to still the cheers.

"And further, I shall propose that he be given a key to the village. Hold the cheers, please, until I'm finished. And tomorrow night when we celebrate the glorious Fourth of July I shall announce it to the whole community . . . I shall be honored to present to our heroic benefactor Marty the key to our great village . . . thank you."

The applause and cheers that followed the Mayor's remarks were deafening.

But Marty pushed his war bonnet up off his eyes and reached up and tugged at the Mayor's sleeve.

The Mayor bent down and asked, "What is it, son?"

"Not tomorrow. Now!"

"What's that? What did he say?" asked the Mayor.

"He wants the key to the village and everything else tonight, I think," said Eddie. "He's leaving tomorrow."

The Mayor straightened up.

"That is a little difficult. Let me see. Maybe I can have that Trustee's meeting right here. I think we have enough Trustees present to pass on it right now."

The Mayor silenced the crowd again with his hand high over his head.

"Mr. Marvel, Captain Jack, and you, Mr. Pearson. There we are, three Trustees. That's a majority. I here and now make the proposal. I move that Marty be made an honorary citizen of the village of Schuyler's Landing with all the privileges that that honor implies, except the right to vote, of course. And furthermore, that we bestow upon him the key to our fair village. What say you? Those in favor say Aye. The Ayes have it."

And the honorable Mayor Sills of the village of Schuyler's Landing took a crumpled paper out of his pocket, wrote something on it and then he signed it with a big flourish.

"Here you are, my lad, that makes it official. We'll send you a proper engraved certificate and a gilded wood reproduction of our village key."

124

Then after the local newspaper man took a flash bulb picture of the Mayor shaking hands with Marty, the ceremony was over. Eddie worried about that picture. Marty's war bonnet slipped down just as the flash went off.

Later when Eddie told his grandmother about Marty's bravery and honors she was delighted.

"Oh, Marty, I'm so proud of you," she cried. "Eddie, where's that pretty little ring Marty gave me last summer? I'll be so proud to wear your ring again, Marty."

Eddie and Marty looked at each other. Then Marty said, "Give new ring tomorrow."

And Marty turned and walked out the kitchen door.

Eddie ran after him and walked with him toward the barn where Marty slept near his space ship.

"Marty," said Eddie, "what was that you used to put out the fire?"

"Anti-Combustion Oxygenized Concentric Ray."

"Oh," said Eddie, "and Marty, look . . . where you gonna get a ring? And where you going tomorrow? I can't go with you, you know. I got to help up at the Rock."

"Will get ring. Will explore Washington, D.C."

Then Marty turned on his special speed and left Eddie far behind him.

The Fourth of July ceremonies up at Washington's Rock lived up to everybody's expectations.

After the speeches and after the Boy Scouts had served lemonade to everybody and the village band played, came the main event of the evening.

Mr. Marvel slowly climbed the steep path up to the top of Washington's Rock. And he alone, while the villagers and Scouts sat around in the meadow below, set off the fireworks.

There were marvelously beautiful rockets, pinwheels and everything else. When he shot off one really astounding rocket that burst and set fiery golden green disks whirling all over the darkened sky, everyone exclaimed, "A-a-h!"

The golden green disks floated gently down and burnt out before they reached the earth.

But there seemed to be one golden green disk higher than all the others that did not come down! That one hovered in the sky over Washington's Rock through the rest of the evening! And it was there until Mr. Marvel lit up the big firework pictures he and Marty had made of George Washington, Abraham Lincoln, Mayor Sills and the great American flag.

When that breathless spectacle had burnt itself out, Eddie, who had been watching that lingering golden green disk, saw it suddenly whirl and shoot off into the velvety skies to join the stars!

Mr. Marvel drove Eddie and his grandmother back from the Fourth of July celebration in his taxi. At Eddie's grandmother's invitation Mr. Marvel came into the kitchen to have a piece of raspberry pie and a glass of milk before he drove home.

The moment they entered the kitchen Eddie shouted, "Look, Grandma . . . Marty's been here!"

There on the kitchen table was a small plaster copy of the Capitol Building in Washington, D.C.! It had a red, white and blue thermometer tacked on its front and on its base were the words, "Souvenir of Washington, D.C.!" The little plaster building rested on a white sheet of paper and by its side lay a pretty Indian beaded ring!

There were some words pencil-printed on the paper:

"Ring for Grandmother . . . Capitol Building for Eddie. Good-bye Friend. Marty."

Eddie's grandmother picked up the beaded ring. It fitted her perfectly. She was very happy.

Mr. Marvel looked at the sheet of paper on which Marty had written his message. The paper had the name and address of a big Washington, D.C. hotel printed on it in one corner.

"The Big Chief sure gets around," said Mr. Marvel.

"He's a fine little boy," said Eddie's grandmother.

And Eddie did not say anything. He just nodded his head.

THE END